ALIEN ABDUCTION

Alex eased the shuttle to starboard. The alien ship she was approaching was big, easily four times the size of the *Michelangelo*.

"Ensign McMichaels," the captain said, raising his voice slightly even though the comm unit would pick up his words even if he whispered them, "if you see anything wrong, if you even get a bad feeling, I want you to turn that shuttle around and jet out of there, is that understood?"

"Aye, captain." Alex's voice was still rock steady.

The boarding party moved away from the shuttle, powered by the small jet packs each one wore. Murdoch killed his own momentum, halting next to the ship. Slowly he reached out and laid his gloved hand on the smooth, black, alien surface. Nothing happened, and everyone started breathing normally again.

"Mr. Murdoch," the captain said, "you have control of the eye. Proceed."

Murdoch powered up the eye. Its four lights came on, and the bottom half of our forward viewscreen on the *Michelangelo* came alive. The black hole of the alien ship's hatch grew larger on the viewscreen. Murdoch's voice said, "Contact in three, two, one—"

His voice cut off. At the moment the eye penetrated the outer hull, the alien ship disappeared, utterly and completely and without any warning whatsoever. And so did all three of the crewmen who were hanging in space next to it....

LARRY SEGRIFF

ALIEN DREAMS

This is a work of fiction. All the characters and events portrayed in this book are fictional, and any resemblance to real people or incidents is purely coincidental.

A Baen Books Original

Baen Publishing Enterprises
P.O. Box 1403
Riverdale, NY 10471

ISBN: 0-671-87860-3

Cover art by Stephen Hickman

First printing, January 1998

Distributed by Simon & Schuster
1230 Avenue of the Americas
New York, NY 10020

Typeset by Windhaven Press, Auburn, NH
Printed in the United States of America

To my daughters, Megan and Caitlin, with love.

Prologue

Lifeless, it drifted silently through the blackness of space. No lights showed along its outer hull, no energy emissions marked it as still functional after all these years. Only one sign, a subtle twisting of the fabric of space, gave any hint of the vast powers it had once commanded.

Time had no meaning out here in the vast empty regions between the stars. How long it had drifted was unimportant. How long it would continue to drift was meaningless. Only the waiting mattered. The waiting and the mission.

Chapter One

I held her hand, feeling the strength that lay beneath her soft, smooth skin. I'd seen those hands in action, watched them flash through the air in quick, heavy punches, seen them curled tightly around the butt of a blaster. But none of that mattered now. She was here, with me, and that was all I cared about.

"Alex," I whispered. I reached out with my free hand and lightly touched her short dark hair, traced the line of her cheekbones, and cupped the back of her head, pulling her toward me.

Her lips smiled, then parted slightly as she leaned forward to kiss me . . .

"Am I boring you, Mr. Jenkins?" Lt. O'Malley's voice cut across my thoughts, pulling me out of Alex's embrace and back into the real world of the Space Guard.

I shook my head, trying frantically to recall what the lieutenant had been saying just before my mind drifted away.

"I'm sorry, sir," I said.

We were three weeks out of Brighthome, still a couple of weeks away from the *Michelangelo*'s regular patrol sector—she had been one of the ships called in early to support the sting operation against the pirates—and Lt. O'Malley was tutoring me on spatial mechanics. It was all pretty basic stuff so far, but necessary if I wanted to be a pilot in the Space Guard. And I most definitely *did* want to be a pilot.

I'd flown an old, reconditioned Space Guard runabout for the last few years on Brighthome, and that had given me my first real taste of space. My next goal was to fly the *Michelangelo* herself.

The role of pilot was one of the most important assignments on board a Space Guard ship—or any vessel, for that matter. There were all sorts of computer systems that could safeguard the ship, make sure that pilot error didn't cause the ship to fly too close to a sun, or come out of hyperspace too deep in a gravity well, but it still took a human to run the ship. Especially a ship of war. There were simply too many unknowns, too many things that might happen, from power failures to navigation error to pirate ships launching sneak attacks. No computer program, no matter how sophisticated, could be prepared for them all.

Which was why the pilot, like the other humans on board, would never be replaced by computers, but that wasn't why I wanted to fly. My dreams were simpler. On Brighthome, flying had been a sort of freedom for me, a brief period where I could have the illusion of being on my own, away from the proctors and the teachers and the other kids. And I'd found that I loved to fly. I was good at it, too, with a natural feel for it, and I knew that, above all, I wanted to pilot the *Michelangelo*.

To do that, however, I also knew that I would have to demonstrate a knowledge of spatial mechanics, navigation, and about half a dozen other disciplines. I'd studied most of these at the Brighthome Youth Center, "Penal Colony to the Stars," as Jamie and I had liked to think of it, but the Guard didn't care about that. My knowledge of these matters had to be up to Guard standards, and so the captain had assigned Lt. O'Malley to evaluate me and to tutor me in any areas where I needed help.

The problem was that O'Malley, who was only a couple of years older than me, had automatically dismissed everything I'd learned on Brighthome and had started my education at the very beginning, rehashing material I'd learned more than two years before.

We were in one of the briefing rooms one deck below the bridge. The table we sat at had seats enough to hold a dozen officers comfortably, with a small computer console built into the tabletop at each place. There were holo units mounted on the walls at both ends for displaying battle plans, system schematics, realtime views from any of the ship's ports, or whatever else the briefing officer chose to call up. Right now the screens were blank.

Around us, the room was silent except for the near-soundless whisper of air as the recyclers scrubbed and replenished the atmosphere on board. There was also a *feeling* of sound, a sense of power and a hint of the engines that drove us through hyperspace.

But the thing that had been hardest to get used to was the complete lack of smell on board. With approximately three hundred fifty crewmen on the *Michelangelo*, our air scrubbers had to be in top condition at all times.

The lieutenant looked at me. His brown hair was cut short in the style of the Guard, and he could be nice enough when he wanted. It was just that during these tutoring sessions he didn't seem to want to.

"I asked you," Lt. O'Malley said, his voice scathing and sharp, "to tell me which laws are most important to a Space Guard pilot."

I looked at him. It was a trick question. It had to be. He'd said "Space Guard pilot," which could be interpreted two ways. Which laws were most important, the laws of society that a Guardsman is sworn to uphold, or the laws of physics that a pilot can never ignore?

"The laws of physics," I said. "A pilot who ignores those is dead, and it's tough to uphold the laws of humanity when you're dead."

He nodded, and I could have sworn his lips twitched into the beginnings of a smile. "Very good," he said. "And *which* laws of physics are the most important to a pilot?"

That was easy, though I suspected it was another trick question. The obvious answer was Einstein's Law of General Relativity, which contained the secrets of interstellar space flight. But that had to be the wrong answer. "The laws of thermodynamics," I said. "Relativity will get you from system to system, but a pilot who forgets the three laws won't live to reach the surface of a planet."

O'Malley nodded, and this time I was sure he was smiling.

"Very good," he said.

I looked at him again. "My last physics instructor was Mr. Forrester," I said, "but that was a cover. I understand he is an active colonel in the Guard." I didn't mention that one of my other teachers, the man who'd taught me to fly—including most of what I knew about spatial mechanics—had been a full-fledged pirate.

The lieutenant grinned. "Well," he said. "That would explain it." He sobered, then, and went on with the lessons, but I must have passed some sort of test because he left the basic stuff and things got more interesting. I put Alex out of my mind and concentrated on what the lieutenant was saying.

Chapter Two

The stars lay scattered before me like jewels on black velvet. I had turned down the lights, so that I didn't see my reflection on the viewscreen before me.

This was my place. Back on Brighthome, I had a cavern I'd discovered, a place where I could get away from the other kids, away from the routine of that place, away from the pressures and the tensions and the troubles. Here on the *Michelangelo*, the routine was different, as were the pressures and the tensions and the troubles, but the result was the same: I needed a place of my own, a place where I could be alone, with a view that could distract me and a silence that could hold all my thoughts.

This was that place.

It was an old war room, once used to brief junior officers back when the pirates were more aggressive, and more numerous. I didn't know if the *Michelangelo* herself dated back that far, but I'd learned that her design did . . . and I was glad of it.

The *Michelangelo* was a cruiser, not the largest ship in service but far from the smallest. Over a hundred meters long, she had ample room for her crew of nearly three hundred fifty Guardsmen, and she fairly bristled with weapons and scanners. Needle-shaped, she was designed for space flight, not atmospheric conditions. Travel to the surface was done by the half-dozen shuttles she normally carried.

But I wasn't there to think about the ship or her mission, I reminded myself. I was there to get away from such thoughts, to avoid my new and overwhelming responsibilities.

The holo unit was set to show the view from one of the aft ports. Already Brighthome's sun had faded into the background, just one more jewel in the dazzling display before me.

I reached out toward the screen, tracing patterns among the stars. Jamie and I had been on board for three weeks now, but I still couldn't believe it. For so long I had dreamed of being here, on a Guard ship, a member of her crew, and now it was really happening. I could look out upon those stars and wonder what adventures I might find out there, and it was no longer simply a dream. Now it was my future.

I stood there a few moments longer, enjoying the view, lost amid my thoughts, and then I turned and headed back to my quarters. I had a watch on the bridge in an hour or so, and I wanted to relax for a while before reporting in.

I glanced back at the stars once more before leaving. Soon, I thought. Soon I would have to tell Jamie about this place. I'd shared my cave with him, and even though we'd never be allowed to camp out down here, I knew I'd have to share this place.

But not yet.

On that note, I turned once more and headed back to my quarters.

Chapter Three

The wardroom that Jamie and I shared was one example of how far ship design had come over the years. I'd been reading up on nautical history in what spare time I could find, and I'd learned that it was common on old submarines—which were the closest analogy I could find to modern space ships—for the enlisted crew members to share common sleeping areas. Those ancient ships were so crowded that they frequently had to hot bunk—three men sharing the same bunk on a rotating shift, so that one would be hitting the sheets just as another was getting up.

There was none of that on the *Michelangelo*. The room Jamie and I shared was small, with our two bunks stacked, mine on top of his, but it was ours, and that made it special. Our superiors had the right to come in at any time, but even for Apprentice Guardsmen like us they wouldn't normally enter without our permission.

Our computer, like all the workstations on a Guard ship, constantly displayed the time and date in one corner of the screen. It was also set to give off an audible tone at each quarter bell.

Jamie was engrossed in a vid unit when I walked into

our bunk room. That was a sight I'd seen often back on Brighthome, but hardly at all here on the *Michelangelo*, and I had to smile at the familiarity of it. The two of us hadn't been able to spend much time together since coming on board. Our duties kept us busy, and we were both still trying to settle into our new roles. We had changed a lot, he and I, in the three short weeks since we'd left the Youth Center—so much, in fact, that at times Brighthome seemed much farther away than a mere three weeks—but seeing him now, his freckled nose buried in a vid unit, I could believe that some things would never change.

I knew that wasn't true, of course. Given enough time, even the stars themselves would change. But I hoped that as Jamie and I forged our futures together, our friendship at least would stay strong.

"Hey, buddy," I said, pulling myself up onto the top bunk.

Jamie merely grunted and didn't look up from his vid. He wouldn't show me his most recent games, but I knew what he was up to. Back on Brighthome, where most kids' deepest dream was to join up with Old Jack's band of pirates, Jamie'd had a collection of live action pirate games. He'd played them all, and taken their code apart when he'd finished to see if he'd missed any tricks, but he'd always played them as one of the pirates. He wouldn't tell me, but I suspected he was playing all those old games again—but this time he was taking on the role of the Guard.

After a while, Jamie's vid beeped and I knew he'd saved the game. He set it aside and looked up at me.

"Any luck?" he asked.

I'd been thinking about Alex, and it took me a moment to return to the stark reality of our wardroom.

"What?" I asked, rising up on one elbow to look down at him.

He grinned, almost as though he knew what I was

thinking. And maybe he did. He knew me pretty well after several years of bunking together.

"You've been accessing the Guard's databases, haven't you?" he asked.

I nodded.

"Well?"

I shook my head and flopped back down on my bunk. When I'd first made up my mind to join the Guard, I'd accepted one dream but turned my back on another, one I'd held for as long as I could remember . . . which wasn't all that long. Four years earlier, a team of Guardsmen had found me drifting through space in a survival pod. I had no memories, not even a name, and no amount of searching had turned up the slightest hint of who I was or where I'd come from. That lack of background had made some people think that I must have been pirate kin, and earned me some much-needed respect on Brighthome. I didn't believe it, though. In my heart, I knew I wasn't a pirate, and so I'd spent many hours on the library's computer system searching through various databases, hunting for any hint as to who I might have been and what might have happened.

I never found anything, and when I made up my mind to join the Guard I accepted the fact that there were some things I would never know. Or so I thought. Less than a week on board the ship, though, I had been given access to the ship's extensive database, and I'd spent more than a little time going through the files. I'd barely dented the vast store of information. Still, my dream had always been to find that my parents were Guardsmen on some secret assignment, perhaps to infiltrate the pirates, and that my only real hope of finding out what had happened was to gain access to the Guards' own files. Well, I had that access now, and I still hadn't found anything, and the disappointment of that was bitter indeed.

"Hey," Jamie said. "Don't get discouraged, Tom. Let

me know the next time you're planning on doing some work and I'll take a look at your search strategies. Maybe together we can find a way to speed things up a bit."

"Thanks, Jamie," I said, but I didn't intend to take him up on his offer. I couldn't say why, exactly, other than that this was something I had to do myself.

"Say," I said, changing the subject, "when are you on watch next?"

"Fifteen minutes," he said. "I thought I'd get cleaned up and then head out. I'm on the bridge today."

"Me, too," I said, and I didn't have to work at sounding happy. It was unusual for raw recruits like Jamie and me to have the chance to serve our watches on the bridge, and we both knew it. I assumed it had something to do with the success we'd had against the pirates, but whatever the reason we knew that that privilege could be revoked at any time. And the bridge was where we wanted to be.

While Jamie went about getting ready, I let my thoughts slide back to Alex. We'd had so little time together on Brighthome, and we'd seen each other only a few times on board the *Michelangelo*, but I found myself thinking about her more and more.

Ten minutes later Jamie was ready. I rolled off my bunk and hit the floor. Straightening my jumpsuit, I ran my fingers through my hair and checked myself in the full-length mirror beside the door.

"Let's go," I said, and led the way toward the bridge.

Chapter Four

The corridors of the *Michelangelo* were pretty plain. The walls and ceiling had been painted a dull grey and the floors were covered with a matching carpet. Overhead, the lights were recessed behind opaque sheets of an extruded polymer. Every twenty feet or so, the corridor made a pair of short right-angle turns, jogging over a few feet and then turning back. The turns alternated in direction, too, jogging first to the right, then twenty feet later, jogging back to the left. Housings protruded slightly from the walls just before the first of each set of turns. These were emergency features, the turns in the corridor designed to keep the force of a blast from shooting all the way along the ship. The housings themselves contained solid sliding doors that would seal off a section in the event of a hull breach. I found their existence more sobering than comforting, though, because they reminded me that for all the excitement of being in space, there were dangers, too.

Our wardroom was five levels below the bridge, with another seven levels below us. At the end of the hallway stood a heavy metal door that could swing shut in an emergency, blocking off the stairwell. There were others,

12

but our quarters were close to the end of the corridor and not far from this access tube. These doors, unlike the blast doors, were not housed, but hung flush against the wall.

"All right, Jamie," I said. "Time to review. What's the term for the door hanging on the wall there?" Jamie and I hadn't had much trouble adapting to the shipboard routine. Ever since coming to Brighthome, we'd been getting up when they told us to, eating when they told us to, and attending the classes that they told us to, so life as a Guardsman wasn't all that different. What had given us the most trouble was the terms they used. On Brighthome, we'd called a door a door. On the *Michelangelo*, they had different names for almost everything, and so Jamie and I grilled each other every chance we got.

Jamie shot me a grin. Stiffening his back, he snapped off a crisp salute and, still smiling, said, "A hatch, sir, and it's not a wall, sir. The proper term is bulkhead."

I grinned back, mostly at him calling me "sir." We were both of the same rank—Apprentice Guardsmen, the lowest of the low—and the only people who should call either of us "sir" were civilians . . . and even that was optional.

"Very good, swabbie," I said. "And tell me once again, *why* are the proper terms hatches and bulkheads?"

"Tradition, sir," he said.

I nodded. That was the Guard's answer for everything. Terminology dated back to the days when ships travelled on water—in fact, many of the terms and routines related most strongly to the old submarine fleets—and everyday customs dated back even further.

"We're Guardsmen," I said, growing serious for the moment. "Discipline keeps us alive, but tradition keeps us together." That was something Captain Browne had said to us when he first welcomed us on board. I still wasn't sure I knew exactly what he meant, but every day

I served on the *Michelangelo* brought me a little closer
to understanding.

Jamie let me step onto the ladder first. It was still
a bit unnerving. The ladders ran all the way from the
bridge to the bottom deck, with exit hatches at each
level in between. They corkscrewed as they rose through
the ship, one quarter turn for each level, with baffles
built in to the tubes. They were there to cut off fire
and the force of any explosion, but they also made sure
that if you slipped off the ladder you wouldn't fall very
far. Even with the baffles there, though, it still felt a
little odd climbing a seven-story ladder. I would have
preferred taking any of the half-dozen or so elevators
on board, but those were only used for moving wea-
ponry and other large or heavy equipment between
levels. This was a ship of war, and elevators were not
designed for battle, where a loss of power could trap
vital personnel between floors.

"Come on," I said. "Let's see how fast you can make
it to the top."

The bridge level was one of several decks I hadn't had
much chance to explore. There were closed doors lining
the corridor. I knew that some of them were conference
rooms, and the senior officers' lounge, but I had no idea
what most of them were.

We were still a few minutes early, so we took our time
approaching the bridge itself. A minute later, I was glad
we weren't hurrying.

Jamie and I came around the third set of turns, two
short of the bridge, when we heard voices from up ahead.
That was nothing new, and neither of us gave it a thought
as we approached, our footsteps silent on the soft grey
carpet.

We came around the next set of turns and froze. There
were two people up ahead, Alex and some other Guardsman. He had her pinned to the wall, his left hand leaning

against the bulkhead beside her, his right hand resting solidly on her waist.

My first thought was of Burles, the bully back on Brighthome, and how he had accosted Mikey. My hands balled into fists and I started to step forward, but Jamie grabbed my arm and pulled me back.

"Look," he whispered.

I did, and I saw what he meant. For one thing, like Burles, the guy who held Alex was a lot bigger than me. More importantly, however, Alex didn't seem to be struggling at all. Even as I watched, she reached up and touched his face lightly, and then gave him a soft, quick kiss.

I sagged back, retreating around the corner, pulling Jamie with me. I'd seen enough, and I had no desire to eavesdrop on their conversation.

Jamie looked at me, and I could see the sorrow on his face. I had no claim on Alex, and he knew that, just as he knew that she and I had never so much as dated. But he also knew how I felt about her, and he knew what that scene was doing to me.

He didn't say anything. He didn't have to. He just clasped my shoulder in silent support.

"Thanks, buddy," I said.

He nodded. After a minute or so, he gestured to his wrist and said, "Tom, we have to go. Our watch starts any moment."

I nodded and, taking a deep breath, led the way around the corner again. They were gone, but the memory of what I had seen hung in the air like a ghost. I turned my face away from the spot where they had stood and continued on to the bridge.

Chapter Five

The bridge of the *Michelangelo* was like nothing I'd ever seen before coming on board. The control section of the old runabout I'd piloted on Brighthome had been small, having barely room enough for a couple of people to sit, with a big control board stretching between them. But the bridge of the *Michelangelo* was much larger. It was also much colder, with the temperature set at a constant sixty-five degrees Fahrenheit to help keep the personnel alert.

There were no portholes, no direct views of space. Instead, the walls of the bridge were lined with consoles, read-outs, monitors, and viewscreens. The blinking lights and beeping sounds from each device could easily have been overwhelming. They weren't, though. Instead, they all blended together into an almost soothing background, and I could see how it would be possible to garner a lot of information from the various stations in a single glance.

Stepping onto the bridge always gave me a wonderful feeling. It filled me with energy and excitement and made me tingle with the warm sensation of coming home. In the three weeks Jamie and I had been serving on the *Michelangelo*, I'd been on the bridge well over a dozen times, and I'd never failed to experience those feelings. Not until today, that is.

There were two large airlock doors separating the bridge from the hallway outside. When the ship was at general quarters, those doors remained wide open, but during drills or actual battle conditions they slid shut, closing off the bridge from the rest of the ship.

As I passed through those doors, I had no thought for the duties that lay ahead of me, no interest in learning more about flying the *Michelangelo*, and no concern for Captain Browne's opinion of me. All I could think about was Alex, how she had touched that other Guardsman, how she had kissed him.

She was there, on the bridge, sitting at the scanner controls, her usual seat. She didn't turn to look at me as Jamie and I entered, but I couldn't help looking at her.

She'd cut her hair since her days on Brighthome, going with a shorter style that fit into a space suit helmet better, but it was still that same gorgeous shade of brown, and it still made me want to run my fingers through it. She'd traded in her black Brighthome jumpsuit for the light blue jumpsuit of the Guard, and I had to admit that this color looked even better on her.

Jamie elbowed me in the ribs before I could get too lost in my thoughts.

"Look sharp, Tom," he whispered at me. Then, giving me a hard look and a sharp nod, he headed over to his station at the scanner controls.

"Good morning, gentlemen," the captain said.

Captain Browne stood at his station at the rear of the bridge, near where we entered. His was the only post that didn't have a seat. The other six stations—Pilot, Navigation, Detection, Gunnery, Communications, and the little used observer's station—all had padded chairs. But the Command station had no seat, no console, nothing to distract the captain or his off-shift replacement from the job of running this ship.

The captain was maybe forty, with a leathery, weathered face—something I'd wondered about since the first time I'd seen him. There wasn't any weather on a star ship, but he looked the part of a sea captain . . . or a sea pirate.

He was a bulldog of a man, well short of two meters tall but weighing in close to eighty kilos. I'd seen him working out in the ship's gym and I knew there was nothing soft about him. Even his hair, cropped close to his scalp, looked like strands of steel laying against his skin. But for all that, and for the iron will he showed on the bridge, I liked him. I'd seen something of the gentleness that lay beneath his armor, and I was very glad that Jamie and I were serving on his ship.

"Good morning, sir," I said. Jamie echoed me.

Out of the corner of my eye, I saw Ensign Robert Goodnuv, the third shift navigator, stand as Jamie approached. They exchanged a quiet word as Jamie took his seat, and then, with a jaunty wave, Ensign Goodnuv left the bridge.

Jamie had been training at the navigator's console since we first came aboard, and was doing quite well at it. I'd spent my first week at Communications— something I'd had little experience with on Brighthome. I'd learned how to use the three different types of communication systems—intraship, in-system/short range, and the longer range but slower hyperwave comm system.

Shipwide announcements and interpersonnel communications were handled through a closed comm unit. All these broadcasts were automatically recorded and logged into the computer, and we could switch over to standard radio to communicate with Guardsmen in their space suits. The heart of the in-system/short range unit was a powerful, tight beam comm laser, and was used mostly for secure transmissions where we didn't want our signal picked up by any pirates or other eavesdroppers.

It didn't work for broad area transmission, but there were times when it was invaluable.

The third unit, the hyperwave comm system, was the most complex, and the hardest to learn. It sent signals through hyperspace, signals that travelled much faster than our ships could but that still took a long time to cross the vast distances between the stars. I knew that if we sent a signal back to Brighthome, which was three weeks away ship's time, it would take just over three days for our signal to be picked up. Still, we used this system a lot, mostly to send our daily log reports back to Command Central.

I was far from expert in any of the three systems, but I could send an SOS if I had to, and I could operate the Space Guard deciphering machines.

The second week I'd trained on the weapons system, dry-firing the ship's laser cannons at asteroids within the Brighthome system. At that, I'd only used about a quarter of the weapons console. There was more to this ship than I'd seen yet, but the laser cannons alone had impressed me tremendously. This week I was assigned to the Observer's station—more to give me a chance to absorb what I'd already learned than to teach me something specific. Or so I thought.

I liked the Guard's routine. There was no mass exodus as a new watch took over. Instead, they had set their day in staggered shifts. The captain appeared on the bridge at 0600. Jamie and I reported at 0800. The other stations changed watches at other times, all so that there was never an hour where all the bridge personnel was fatigued. I wasn't sure how they handled that in battle. I had the feeling that the first shift personnel might stay on duty longer then, but we hadn't covered that in my training. And, as far as I was concerned, that was a bit of knowledge I hoped I'd never need.

I made an effort to put Alex out of my mind. I was still hurt by what I'd seen, but the time to deal with that was when I was off-shift, not when I was on the bridge. I gave Jamie a wink and a grin to let him know that I was all right, and then headed toward my assigned station. As I did so, I couldn't help glancing over at the Command station, like I always did. That post suited the captain so perfectly, and I couldn't help wondering if I would ever have the chance to stand there. One impossible dream had come true, after all. I was in the Guard. Why not another?

Captain Browne caught my glance, as he always did.

"Mr. Jenkins," he said.

"Sir," I said. Stopping in my tracks, I snapped to attention. The Guard wasn't big on formality; their emphasis was on discipline. They didn't go in much for saluting and parade ground drilling and all that, but God help the Guardsman who left his bunk unmade or allowed her uniform to get a little shabby. A salute wouldn't save your life in space, they figured, but attention to detail just might. Still, Jamie and I were the new kids on the ship and, coming from Brighthome as we did, we'd both figured it wouldn't hurt to try a little harder to make an impression.

Captain Browne stood easily at his station. He had the look that I hoped to have one day, the confidence and physical presence of a born Guardsman. Even without the bright blue jumpsuit with the Space Guard insignia on the left breast, I would have known he was a Guardsman just by the way he carried himself. And the aura of command he wore marked him as a captain even more than the gold braid adorning his suit just above his name patch on the right side of his uniform.

"I understand you're something of a pilot," he said.

I shook my head. "Not by Guardsman standards, sir."

He smiled at that. "I'll be the judge of that, Mr. Jenkins."

"Yes, sir," I said.

I didn't move, and after a moment he said, "I'll be the judge of that *now*, Apprentice."

I still didn't get it. "Sir?" I repeated.

He nodded toward the pilot's station. "That is your seat for today, Mr. Jenkins. It'll be up to you whether you sit there tomorrow as well."

And that's when I got it. Sudden excitement exploded within me. I was going to get to fly the *Michelangelo*!

"Sir!" I said, and I couldn't help myself. I snapped off a salute, spun, and then fairly raced to the pilot's station.

Lt. Lovejoy was the regular pilot for this shift. I'd only spoken with him a few times, but he seemed like a nice guy. He gave me a wink and a smile as he rose from his seat and stepped aside.

I slipped into the chair with a feeling of reverence. The board was similar to the runabout I'd flown at Brighthome, and I'd studied it enough since coming aboard to know what the extra controls did. But this was the first time I'd had them at my fingertips.

Lt. Lovejoy didn't go far. He stayed at my right shoulder, overseeing my every move, ready to counter any mistake I made. A part of me was glad he was there, but for the most part I simply put him out of my mind. This was my shot, my big chance, and I was determined that Lt. Lovejoy would do nothing but watch.

The captain gave me a few moments to orient myself and then he said, "All right, Mr. Jenkins. Let's see what you can do."

To my right, Jamie gave me a grin and a quick thumbs-up and then returned his attention to his board. My own lips twitched in an answering smile. Then the captain started issuing orders and I was too busy to do anything but fly the ship.

I expected the *Michelangelo* to be heavier than the runabout. She—friendly ships of any kind were always female—obviously massed much more than the little shuttle I'd flown, and I assumed she would be less responsive. I was wrong. If anything, the cruiser handled lighter than the runabout, her powerful engines easily overcoming the extra mass.

She handled course changes like a dream, though the first few I did I was a bit heavy-handed on, anticipating more inertial resistance and cutting the angles short to compensate. I'd figured it out by the third one, however, and after that I felt as though I'd been born to fly this ship.

The captain gave me an hour and then turned the controls over to Lt. Lovejoy once more.

"Nice flying, Mr. Jenkins," he said.

"Thank you, sir."

I returned to the observer's station, but I didn't observe much. I spent the rest of the shift remembering how the ship had handled, how the controls had felt beneath my fingers, and looking forward to tomorrow and my next chance to fly this ship.

Chapter Six

Jamie and I left the bridge together. We made it through the double doors and around the first jog in the corridor, just far enough so that the officers on the bridge wouldn't hear us, and I let out a whoop of joy.

Jamie grinned at me and slapped me on the shoulder. "Hey, Tom," he said. "Nice flying, pilot."

I grinned at him. "Just like old times, eh, Jamie?" I said. "You at navigation, me at the helm."

He nodded, and for a moment we were as close as we'd been back on Brighthome.

"So," I said, "I'm starved. You want to get something to eat?" We used to take all our meals together, back at the Youth Center, something we hadn't been able to do much of here.

His grin widened. "Sounds great," he said. "Let's go."

Our mess hall was one deck below our quarters, but on the other side of the ship. It took us close to five minutes to get there, and during that time neither Jamie nor I said much, but I didn't mind. We'd been friends for so long that our silences could be comfortable. Just being together was more important than having interesting things to say.

On Brighthome, the cafeteria had been large enough to hold a couple hundred kids and was pretty noisy during meal times. It was different here. For one thing, with the staggered watches, no more than a quarter of the crew ate at any one time. For another, this was only one of several mess halls on board. The captain had his own private dining room, where he ate with the senior staff. Officers had a cafeteria of their own. And the rest of us were divided up among three different mess halls.

But the food was always good and there was plenty of it, and after standing watch on the bridge you were officially through for the day, which meant that you could linger over your food. Not that most people did. There was an old joke that people who wolfed their food ate like Guardsmen because, like old-time firemen, Guardsmen never knew when they might be called to action and wanted to be sure they got filled up.

Jamie and I entered our mess hall and went straight to the serving line. I'd heard that the officers didn't have to go through a line like this, that they had real waiters and everything, but I didn't believe it. I'd been reading through the different duties on board the *Michelangelo*, and I hadn't seen anyone classified as a waiter.

We had loaded up our plates and were heading toward an empty table in the far corner when I heard my name called out.

"Jenkins! Over here!"

I turned and saw Lt. O'Malley sitting with a couple of other junior officers. There was one empty place, and the lieutenant was waving me over.

I turned to Jamie. "That's Lt. O'Malley," I said. "He's been tutoring me on spatial mechanics."

Jamie gave me a weak grin, but I could see the hurt in his eyes. "It's all right," he said. "I understand."

"Forget it," I said. "I don't have to eat with him."

He shook his head. "It's all right," he repeated. "He's a lieutenant. He outranks me." He grinned again, and this time there was real humor in it. "Besides," he added, "we can get together later, right?"

I nodded. "You got it, buddy," I said, punching him lightly in the arm. "Thanks, Jamie."

He went off to eat by himself, and I headed over to meet the lieutenant.

"Jenkins," O'Malley said as I set my tray down next to his, "I'd like you to meet Lts. Wu and Freeman, two of the best shuttle pilots on board the *Michelangelo*."

Lt. Freeman chuckled. "Don't let him kid you, Jenkins," he said. "Wu and I are two of the *last* shuttle pilots on board. We transferred most of the rest over to the *Daedalus* to help run escort while they take Old Jack back for trial."

Lt. O'Malley waved a hand. "True," he said, "but why do you think Captain Browne kept these two behind? He figured if he was going to be down to just a few pilots, he wanted them to be the best he could get." He motioned for me to sit down. "They fly the same kind of ship you earned your flames on," he said when I was seated. "Once I'm convinced you're ready, I'll be turning you over to them for more advanced training. They'll be the ones to determine whether your flames are up to Guardsman standards."

I nodded. "It's a pleasure to meet you both," I said, shaking their hands.

They made an odd pair. Lt. Wu was a smallish woman, with straight black hair and an Asian cast to her features. Freeman, on the other hand, was a large man with dark skin and short, wiry black hair. They seemed comfortable together, though, and I could tell just by looking at them that they were good friends.

"So," Lt. Wu said. Her voice was slightly higher than I'd expected, but there was strength in it, too. "O'Malley here tells us you flew a runabout for a number of years?"

I nodded. "An old one," I said, "but I understand it was Guard issue at one time."

"What kind of systems did it have?" Lt. Freeman asked. His voice fit him perfectly, deep and strong, and though he kept the volume down I could tell from the timbre that it would carry as far as he needed it to.

"Minimal," I said. "Communications, helm and navigation. No weapons at all, of course, but it did have both a modified pulse radar and a hyperwave detection grid. Not that we had much chance to use those," I added with a small grin.

Wu was frowning. "Sounds like the kind of reconditioned bird we send to Brighthome," she said.

My smile faded. So O'Malley hadn't told them, and I had just announced it like the idiot I was.

"It was," I said. "I spent four years there." I didn't add anything further. If they were interested in why I was there, they'd ask. If not, they probably wouldn't believe me anyway.

Neither of the lieutenants moved, but I could feel them sort of stiffen and withdraw.

O'Malley shot me a look I couldn't read and then said, "He was trained by Colonel Forrester, who I hear is still active."

Again they didn't move, but I could feel them thaw somewhat, and I made a mental note to look the colonel up in the database. That was the second time his name had worked a minor magic on my behalf, and I was getting very curious about his reputation in the Guard.

"Well," Lt. Freeman said, "I guess it's up to you, O'Malley. If you pass him on, we'll give him a chance."

The conversation turned to other things, then, fuel consumption rates, deceleration maneuvers, stories from the Academy, and shipboard gossip. I knew enough to keep my head down and my mouth shut, except for shovelling in bite after bite.

It was interesting, and I was looking forward to the challenge I'd just been handed, but as I ate I couldn't help being aware of Jamie, who sat in the corner with his shoulders hunched and his back to me.

I had a lot of challenges to face all of a sudden—proving myself to the captain, to Lt. O'Malley, and now to these two. But most of all, I knew, I had to prove myself to me.

Jamie ate quickly, and left as soon as he'd finished. I watched him take his tray back and leave, but he never once looked over at me. I frowned, and once he'd gone I bent down over my food and concentrated on what the officers were saying.

Chapter Seven

The next several days went by in a blur. I got to fly the *Michelangelo* again on each of my watches on the bridge, for longer periods each time. Lt. O'Malley accelerated my studies to the point where they were interesting and even challenging, which meant that I had little time to spend on my own researches, or with Jamie.

I did see Alex a couple of times, but I didn't get the chance to speak with her. She was alone both times, though, which gave me some small sense of satisfaction.

I bumped into her again on the morning of our twenty-fifth day on board the *Michelangelo*. I was heading into the mess hall for breakfast as she was coming out.

"Tom," she said, her face brightening.

"Hi, Alex," I said. "How're you doing?"

She shrugged. "Busy. This route isn't travelled much—" she grinned and winked at me "—not many Guard ships fly in and out of Brighthome, so I'm spending most of my off-watch time down in Cartography, interpreting the data sent down from the bridge. The captain has asked everyone who's checked out on the scanners to put in extra time on this. But that's tradition, right? Never miss a chance to update your charts. You never know when you might need them."

I nodded. I wanted to say something else, anything that would keep her there a moment longer, but she spoke before I could think of anything.

"I'm glad we ran into each other, Tom," she said. "I need to get you started on your physical training, but I haven't had time to set it up."

"That's okay," I said.

"No," she said. "It's not. This is important, and it's past time for you to begin. I'll tell you what: why don't you report to the gym at fourteen hundred hours today. Will you be off shift by then?"

I nodded.

"Good. What about Jamie?"

"I don't know," I said. "Our schedules are crossed, and we haven't seen much of each other lately. I'm not sure what time his shift ends."

She frowned, but only for a moment. "Okay," she said. "We'll worry about him later. If you see him, though, ask him to come along, will you? Oh, and wear something loose fitting, and don't eat right before coming down. You won't work out too hard today, but I don't want you cramping up."

"All right," I said.

"Great. Listen, Tom, I've got to run. Don't forget, though, okay?"

I grinned. I couldn't help myself. The closest thing to a date she and I had ever had, and she was worried I might forget? "I won't," I promised.

She gave me a smile and a wave and was gone. I watched her go, sappy grin on my face, and when she had disappeared around the first turn I went and got myself some food. I had no idea what they were serving for breakfast that day, but it was the best food I'd eaten in weeks.

✦   ✦   ✦

I managed to stay focussed during my watch and didn't
fly us into anything—not that there was much to fly into
out in the interstellar reaches we were currently crossing,
but at least I didn't embarrass myself. More importantly,
I didn't give Captain Browne any reason to revoke my
flying privileges.

I was hungry when I got off shift but, mindful of her
words, I didn't eat more than a light snack. I changed
into an old jumpsuit—one with the Brighthome patch
carefully cut away from the left shoulder—and waited
anxiously for 1400 hours to roll around.

I got there early, about fifteen minutes before I was
supposed to show up, and found the gym empty. I hadn't
been there before, but it was big enough that I didn't
have any trouble finding it. It was in the very center of
the ship, right next to the shooting range.

The gym itself was a large, rectangular room running
along the central axis of the ship. The ceiling was higher
than anywhere else on board I'd seen, making it seem
even bigger than it was.

It was strange, walking into that empty room. There
was no smell—the air scrubbers on board worked too
well for that—but it was almost as if the *memory* of all
the past blood and sweat and tears still hung in the air.
There was also no echo, even though the room was large
enough to provide for good reverberation. The mats
lining much of the walls softened the small noises I made
walking around.

I was surprised to find the room empty. With the
staggered shifts we ran, most of the crew was off duty
at any given moment, and I'd expected to find several
of them down here, working out and killing time. I was
glad they weren't, however. I didn't really want an
audience for my first workout, and I wondered if that
was just coincidence or if Alex had put the word out,
asking people to stay away for the next hour or so.

I shrugged, then, and put the thought out of my mind. However it had happened, I was thankful for it. And, with a little time on my hands, I decided to explore the gym a bit before Alex arrived.

At the far end, the floor was covered with thick mats and I assumed that was where we would work out. The area just before the mats was made into a small *salle d'armes*, with fencing strips laid out on the floor, and I killed some time looking at the racked swords and masks. I was careful not to touch the blades, though. None of the swords looked sharp, but I didn't know anything about fencing and I didn't want to risk damaging them or me.

The rest of the gym held some equipment I'd seen before, and a few devices that were totally new to me. I'd never been all that big on working out, but I was fascinated by much of what I saw. There was a bank of controls near the door that allowed anyone to vary the gravity within the gym, making their workouts easier or much more difficult. I didn't touch these controls, but I saw that the settings ranged from zero up to three and a half g's.

Working out with free weights would be interesting in zero-g, I realized. After all, the weights would still have their same mass, but without the ship's artificial gravity pulling them down all the time, you'd be able to work them in some interesting positions, really concentrating on specific muscle groups and even individual muscles.

I assumed that there was another benefit to the variable gravity, as well: no one had mentioned it to me yet, but I realized that the gym would be a great place to practice working outside the ship. I had the feeling that at some point in my training I would be down here in the gym, in my space suit, getting used to wearing it and to working in a zero-g environment.

I wasn't looking forward to that. I'd experienced weightlessness a time or two, and had not enjoyed it.

Quickly, I pushed that thought from my mind and went back to inspecting the various devices.

Perhaps the most interesting piece of equipment, at least to me, was the ship's pride and joy: an augmented body suit, too thin to function as a space suit but fitted with tiny motors to provide variable resistance at every joint. Instead of a standard visor, it had a wraparound computer monitor that could be set to display any one of several dozen interactive programs.

With this suit and the right program, I—or anyone else who wanted to use it—could picture myself in almost any environment: wrestling in the first Olympiad back in ancient Greece, swimming the English Channel, or practically anything else I could find a program for. There were additional devices to add to the sense of actually being there—a stationary bicycle, a treadmill, a climbing wall, and a few others—but the suit was what made it all real.

I could even fight in that suit, pitting myself against opponents in every art form, from rank novice to the greatest masters throughout history. But I wasn't interested in that. I doubted I would ever be good enough to need that kind of challenge, and I had the feeling that I would always rather practice with a real person.

Alex showed up right on time. She wore a white martial arts outfit and I couldn't help noticing how good she looked in it. She didn't give me much time to enjoy the view, however. As soon as she came in she waved me over to the mats, gave me a quick smile, and started right in.

"Do you know anything about hand-to-hand combat, Tom?" she asked.

I shook my head. "Not really."

She nodded. "Okay, then we'll start with the basics. The first thing is to stretch. For now, you probably won't be able to punch or kick hard enough to pull anything— though it may feel that way as you exercise muscles you didn't even know you had—but you'll want to get into the habit of stretching. In fact, you should do this every day, right after you get up, whether you're planning on working out or not."

She showed me several different stretching techniques. Some of them I'd seen before, mostly in physical education classes on Brighthome, but many of them were new to me.

"Do this slowly," she said. "You should spend at least fifteen minutes stretching."

I nodded, but I wasn't really paying much attention to what she was saying. I was too distracted by trying not to stare. She was more limber than I was, and a lot more interesting to look at.

We stretched for fifteen minutes or so and then she showed me some very basic moves: how to stand, how to throw a straight punch, how to block a fist coming at my face, things like that. We didn't talk much, except about what we were doing, but I realized that I was having more fun than I'd had the entire time I'd been on board.

"Good," she said after a while. "I think you're ready."

"For what?" I asked.

"To spar."

I looked at her. I could still remember how fast her hands had flashed when she'd taken Burles apart.

"I'll try to take it easy on you," I said, grinning.

She didn't smile back. "Oh, not me," she said. "I've found it's better for new students to work with opponents bigger than themselves, with longer reach and more power. It teaches you your mistakes faster than anything else, and forces you to develop good form."

I frowned. "Not you? Then who?"

She smiled and pointed behind me, toward the main entrance to the gym. "Him," she said. "Tom, I'd like you to meet your sparring partner, Ensign Will Davies."

I turned and felt my stomach turn to ice. The guy

walking through the door was big all right, and moved with a confidence that mirrored hers, but that wasn't what caused my hands to curl reflexively into fists.

Ensign Davies was the guy I'd seen kissing Alex the other day.

He walked over casually, nodded at me, gave Alex a wink and, without so much as a word, he threw a punch at my face.

I didn't move. I couldn't. His punch was too fast, and I was frozen by the sudden dark anger that had risen up within me.

His fist stopped less than a quarter inch from my nose. We stood there, motionless, for the space of three or four heartbeats. At last he quirked a little half grin, glanced over at Alex, and said, "I can see we've got some work to do."

Alex looked at me, an unreadable expression on her face. I didn't meet her gaze for long, however. There were too many conflicting emotions churning inside me, and I didn't want her to get a glimpse of them.

My limbs thawed and we began to spar. Ensign Davies shuffled around me, turning me in a constant, slow circle, occasionally snapping off lightning quick kicks or punches. Alex stood at my back, whispering brief instructions, correcting my form with a touch here or a push there. After ten or fifteen minutes I had progressed to where I was blocking some of his slower attacks, but none of my counters came anywhere close to getting past his guard.

All in all, we sparred for maybe half an hour. At the end, I was exhausted and drenched with sweat. Ensign Davies didn't even look winded, and I hated him even more for that.

"Okay," he said, stepping back and bowing to me. "Not bad for a first time. Go back to your quarters, rest up, do some more stretching later, and meet me here tomorrow at this same time, all right?"

I nodded and, at Alex's urging, returned his bow, though mine was much quicker and shallower than his.

He winked at her and walked away. I watched him go, feeling a tide of emotion pulling at me. On the one hand, as much as I hated to admit it, he seemed like a nice enough guy, and he had certainly been patient with me. On the other hand, I'd seen him kissing Alex.

When he had gone, she turned to look at me. "Are you all right, Tom?" she asked.

I nodded, but she didn't let it go at that.

"I was getting worried about you," she said. "Do you know that you haven't spoken a word since he walked in?"

I looked at her and felt some of the stiffness within me relax. "Just nervous, I guess," I said, giving her a weak little grin. "This has all been pretty overwhelming, you know."

"This class, you mean?" she asked.

"Everything," I said. "The Space Guard, the *Michelangelo* . . ." *You*, I wanted to add, but couldn't. "Everything," I repeated.

She sighed. "I know, Tom," she said. "I wish—" She shrugged, then, and changed the subject without finishing the thought. "Listen, Will was right. The best thing for you now is to get some rest. You'll be stiff and sore later, but stretching will help, and in a few days you'll be able to do this without the pain. Oh, and you should go down to Supply and have them issue you a gi like mine. They're more comfortable than that old jumpsuit, and more appropriate, too."

I nodded. "Alex," I said. "Thanks. For everything."

She smiled at me, and touched my cheek lightly, and then she turned and walked away. I waited until she had gone and then I turned and looked out over the gym. All the conflicting emotions within me had combined with my exhaustion and resolved themselves into an inexplicable sadness. I couldn't explain it, but it washed over me as I stood there feeling my pain.

After a while, I turned and headed back to my bunk. Maybe things would look brighter after a long, hot shower. I didn't really believe it, but it was all I could think of to do.

Chapter Eight

The comm unit in my quarters was flashing when I walked in, telling me that there was a message waiting. I peeled off my sweaty jumpsuit and hit the PLAY button as I headed toward the shower.

I figured it was Jamie. I was wrong. It was Lt. O'Malley, instructing me to come down to our briefing room as soon as I could. He'd logged the message nearly half an hour ago. I hit the ACKNOWLEDGE button and kept walking toward the shower. If it had been urgent, the lieutenant would have found me in the gym. Besides, whatever he wanted, I wasn't about to show up all sweaty and smelly.

I did hurry, though, and was out of the shower in under five minutes. Pulling on a fresh uniform, I ran a comb through my hair and headed out the door.

Lt. O'Malley was waiting for me, and he wasn't alone. Lts. Wu and Freeman were with him.

I hurried in, mumbling apologies, but Lt. O'Malley waved them away. "Don't worry about it, Jenkins," he said. "You're off-shift and this was unscheduled."

"Thank you, sir," I said, but he waved that off, too.

"Apprentice," he said, "you remember my friends here."

I nodded. "Pilots, sir," I said. "We met in the mess hall the other day."

He nodded. "And you remember what I said."

I nodded again. "Absolutely, sir."

He smiled. "Well, the time has come. You've been doing very well, and I think you're ready to move out of the classroom. What do you think?"

My eyes lit up. "Are you serious, sir?" I asked.

His grin widened. "Absolutely," he said. Wu and Freeman chuckled, but their humor was good-natured and I didn't mind. "Come on," he said, and led the way out the door.

Seven minutes later we were seated inside one of the *Michelangelo*'s runabouts. As instructed, I took the pilot's seat. O'Malley took weapons control, though I noticed he only gave his board a perfunctory check. Lt. Freeman sat down at navigation, to my right, his hands moving with the confidence of long experience. Lt. Wu took up a spot directly behind me so that both she and Lt. Freeman could watch my actions.

This was the first time I'd sat at the controls of one of these shuttles, but most of the controls of the shuttle were familiar to me. The ships on board the *Michelangelo* were all newer and in much better shape than the ones I'd flown back on Brighthome, but the configurations were all pretty much the same. There were some differences, though—"Space Guard Specials" that had been removed when the old runabouts were decommissioned. I'd read up on them, of course, in what little spare time I'd been able to find, and I knew that the biggest among these were the weapons.

Space Guard shuttles had two primary weapon systems. The first, and the one I was least likely to ever use, was the bank of missiles each shuttle carried. These were called ship killers because they were designed to do just that: penetrate the armored hull of even the biggest and best protected ship and direct the full force of their explosion inward, through the ship, destroying much of the equipment and killing almost all of the people on board.

The missiles had chemical reaction engines. Whatever fuel still on board at the moment of impact simply added to the force of the explosion. Each shuttle—including the one I would be flying—had ten of these on board.

The ship killers were powerful weapons, but they were a Guardsman's last choice. Bombs in space were always dangerous. Even with their cutting edge guidance systems and their failsafes, there was always the chance that a missile like this would explode too early, impacting on the hull of a ship or even missing the target ship entirely. That could be a problem because shrapnel, like any other moving object, would travel forever in space—or at least until it was stopped by something else. The danger with the ship killers was that even if the missiles performed perfectly, our own ships could be damaged by shrapnel or debris from the explosion. Which is why the blasters were the preferred weapon for most Guardsmen.

Based on the same principle as the hand weapons we carried, the blasters were essentially industrial-strength lasers, but with a broader beam. There were no alternate settings, no "stun" functions on these weapons. They were designed to kill, or to disable. Our hand weapons fired a two-inch-wide beam, and could be set to pulse or for continuous fire. The ship-based blasters fired a beam eight inches across, and didn't have pulse capability.

A shuttle's blasters could take the armor right off a ship. A direct hit from one of these would burn off a full two feet of armor plating in less than five seconds, and the full-size weapons mounted on the *Michelangelo* herself were even more powerful—which was why both pirate and Guardsmen ships had to be quick and agile. The idea was to not let a blaster beam continue to fall on the same area on your ship for more than a few moments.

There was also a single, smaller blaster unit. This one was more like the hand-held weapons in that it fired a tighter—but much more powerful—beam. Our hand weapons were designed to work against people; these were designed to carve through the armor plating on a ship. It was delicate work, and almost never used in battle, but this weapon was our best chance of disabling an enemy ship without destroying it. With the added precision of this tighter beam, we could cut through cables or disable engines—but not easily, especially in the heat of battle.

And that was pretty much all I knew about the weapons on board the shuttles. They had other surprises, I was sure, but I didn't really need to know more than what they did and how to fire them. I was the pilot, after all, and Space Guard shuttles were designed to be manned by more than one person. In a pinch, I could operate everything—including the weapons—from my consoles, but there weren't many circumstances where that would come up.

I grinned, then, thinking about that. I was a mere apprentice. There weren't many circumstances where I was going to be flying a shuttle at all, much less in a situation where her weapons might be needed.

And that was fine with me. I wanted to fly, and to explore. I'd leave the fighting to others.

Still grinning, I turned back to the controls and started my pre-flight check.

"All right, Apprentice," Lt. O'Malley said. "Show us what you've got."

"Yes, sir," I said. I ran through my pre-flight check. I was itching to get going, but I knew better than to rush through this part. Instead, I forced myself to take my time and do it right.

"Light your engines," Lt. Wu said, when I had completed my check.

"Aye," I said, acknowledging the order. At my touch,

the ship came to life quickly and easily, and I smiled as the old, familiar feelings swept over me.

"My board shows green," I said.

"Open the hangar door," she said.

I froze. "Sir?" I said.

"Is there a problem, Apprentice?" she asked. "Didn't your Brighthome instructors show you the hangar door controls?"

"They did, sir—" I began.

"Then carry out my instruction, Apprentice."

I sighed. "No, sir," I said.

Beside me, Lt. Freeman turned to look at me, an unreadable expression on his face.

"Explain yourself, Apprentice Jenkins," Lt. Wu said. "And make it good."

"We're still in hyperspace, sir," I said, gesturing toward the display to my right. "This runabout, unlike the *Michelangelo* herself, is only equipped with a chemical reaction drive. She's not built for hyperspace, sir, and can't handle it. I don't have the math skills to describe what would happen if I opened that hangar door right now, but I do know that we would not survive it."

Lt. Freeman chuckled. Behind me, Lt. Wu said, "Very good, Apprentice."

I relaxed, but only slightly. "That was a test, wasn't it?" I asked.

"Of course," she said. "And you passed."

I frowned, not satisfied by what she'd said. For one thing, it had been too easy.

Lt. Freeman could see my face, and he must have read something of what I was feeling. "Perhaps you don't understand," he said. "We weren't testing your piloting skills. That will come later. We knew that you would be able to tell that we were still in hyperspace, and from what O'Malley here says we assumed that you knew what would happen if you pressed that button. What we were testing was to see how you would handle receiving an order like that—and, as Lt. Wu said, you passed the test."

I nodded, but I still wasn't satisfied. "What would have happened if I'd pressed that button?" I asked.

Lt. Freeman grinned. "Nothing," he said. "The *Michelangelo* has safeguards in place that would prevent the hangar doors from opening while we're in hyperspace."

Of course, I thought.

"You couldn't know that," he said. "And you did exactly what you should have—you put the safety of your crewmates before the need to follow orders."

I didn't agree. He said I couldn't have known that, but he was wrong. I had full access to all the ships' specs. I could have checked the shuttles out more thoroughly earlier, learning all their features, all their safety features, not just the ones I wanted to know about—and I should have. And if I had, I would have known about the safeguards.

Of course, if I had, I would have gone ahead and pressed that button when ordered to, knowing that it wouldn't have worked. Which meant that if I had done my homework properly I would have failed their test— but I would have passed my own, and that was more important to me.

"Power down," Lt. Wu said. "That's all for today. Tomorrow we'll start you on the simulator, but for now you look pretty beat. Get some rest, Apprentice, and we'll see you tomorrow."

I was disappointed. I would have preferred to keep working, to have the chance to redeem myself, but I did as she instructed. That wasn't the kind of order I could disobey.

Tomorrow, I thought. Tomorrow I would do better. Tomorrow I would really show them what a kid from Brighthome could do.

Chapter Nine

By dinnertime my muscles had started to stiffen. I moved through the mess hall slowly, trying not to bump into anyone, and for once I was glad I didn't see anyone I knew. I hadn't heard from Jamie all day and didn't know where he might be. The lieutenants had probably eaten already, and there was no sign of Alex.

The meal was some sort of casserole, and I was almost as hungry as I was tired. I went through two full plates, and then grabbed some fruit to take back to my bunk with me, but I didn't head back there right after dinner. Instead, I decided to try and get in a little research time.

The library on the *Michelangelo* was nothing like what I'd grown used to on Brighthome. There were no books, for one thing. Everything was stored in the computer, and though their collection was extensive I missed being able to hold books in my hands. On Brighthome, I'd fallen in love with the printed word. I liked the weight of a book, I liked the smell of mildew and old ink. I even liked turning the pages, that moment of anticipation as I paused during a tense scene to turn to the next page.

We all had our addictions, I realized. Jamie had his computers and his vid units. I had my books and my flying. And Alex—well, she had the Guard, I guessed, her traditions and her discipline and her bonds with her crewmates. But I couldn't help wondering what else she had, what she did in her spare time when she was alone and off shift. I couldn't know, of course, but that didn't stop me from speculating.

I smiled at the direction my thoughts had gone. I'd come down here to search for my past and, as always, I'd ended up daydreaming about my future. Shaking my head, I turned back to my console and made an effort to concentrate.

The library here consisted of a small room with half a dozen computer stations, each in its own small carrel. There was no librarian, no one to guide me through the immense storehouse of information available through those workstations, but that was all right. It had taken me a little while to familiarize myself with this system, but I'd quickly grown comfortable with it. Now all I needed were some results.

I was using a different search strategy than the ones I'd developed with the help of Jamie and Mr. Murphy, the librarian on Brighthome. There I had refined various ways to search out reports of missing persons. I was looking for my parents—and for myself—and had spent countless hours searching through old news items, looking for some clue as to where I might have come from. I never found one, but I ended up with some powerful, efficient search routines.

I hadn't used any of those here. The first time I sat down at this terminal I had stumbled across something very interesting. I had requested a general report, a listing of all Guardsmen who had disappeared, and who were still listed as missing. I gave it no other parameters, not even limiting it to the past five years, and the list it had turned up was extensive. Since then, I'd been reading up on the missing Guardsmen, and in the process learning quite a bit about the history and traditions of the Space Guard.

The first Guardsman to ever go missing was a Lt. Jane Katzman. She was the pilot of a single ship, the old-time scout ships that opened up the very first travel lanes. She'd headed off into the great unknown and was never heard from again. Some of the later files had notations in them, later findings that shed new light on old disappearances, or sometimes just speculation on what might have happened. Hers had nothing like that. She had simply disappeared, leaving nothing behind to speculate on.

There were quite a few "Missing—Presumed Dead" listings from battles with the pirates. Entire ships had vanished after engaging with the enemy. The lack of debris indicated that the ships had probably been boarded, even though the Guard itself still maintained that space piracy should be physically impossible.

The most interesting one I'd found so far was a lowly ensign who'd disappeared from his ship more than thirty years before. His name was Jack Finnegan, and there was a notation in his file that he was suspected of having gone over to the pirates. There was nothing else listed about him, but I couldn't help wondering. The leader of the pirates—who, if the rumors were right, was even now in custody on board the *Daedalus*, under very tight security, on his way to trial—was called "Old Jack." It was probably mere coincidence, but I found it interesting that more than thirty years ago someone might have started out a lowly ensign in the Space Guard and ended up the leader of the pirates. Wouldn't Jamie get a kick out of that?

I called up the list I'd stored in the system and continued reading, picking reports at random and deleting them when I'd finished. This was an inefficient system, I knew, but I was enjoying myself, and some of the stories were interesting enough to make me forget about my aches and pains for a while.

Still smiling at the thought of Jack Finnegan, I selected a name and started reading.

Chapter Ten

I woke up the next morning stiff and sore. My legs didn't want to straighten all the way, and just standing up was painful.

Alex had told me that stretching would help. She was probably right about that, too, but at the moment the mere thought of moving was painful. There was no way I could lift my arms up over my head, or do any of the other exercises she'd shown me yesterday.

Jamie cracked one eye open as I grunted and groaned my way down the ladder at the foot of my bed.

"Rough night?" he asked.

I shook my head. "Self-defense training," I said. "My second lesson is this afternoon. Want to join me?"

He chuckled. "What, so I can walk like a hunchback, too? No, thanks."

I glared at him, but I didn't really blame him. I wished I could get out of it, too, especially now that I knew I'd be sparring with Davies, but I didn't have any choice. And I suspected Jamie didn't either. Sooner or later, he'd be feeling just like I was. And maybe I'd get to be the one who sparred with him.

That thought cheered me as I shuffled off to take a long, hot shower.

I didn't get any sympathy out of Lt. O'Malley, either. He took one look at me as I made my slow and careful way into the briefing room and asked me if it hurt to think. When I told him no, he grinned and said, "Then let's get started."

He grilled me pretty good for a couple of hours, and I found both comfort and distraction in the finer points of hyperwaves and hyperspace. When we were done, he clapped me on the shoulder, reminded me of the simulation sequence I had scheduled for later that day with the inseparable Lts. Freeman and Wu, and then let me go.

I thanked him, grabbed some food in the mess hall, stretched a bit in my quarters, and then headed up for my watch on the bridge.

Jamie was there ahead of me, which probably meant that his watch had started an hour or two before mine. Alex was seated beside him, handling the scanner controls like she was born to sit there. She glanced at me as I came in, a look of sympathy on her face, and then turned back to her board.

Jamie grinned at me, his freckled face full of delight, and I shot him a dirty look before taking my place beside Lt. Lovejoy.

"It'll pass," the lieutenant said as I took my seat. "We've all been there."

"Thanks," I said, "but I'm trying not to think about it."

He chuckled and then he was back to all business, giving me a report on our position, course, and speed before turning the controls over to me.

"Nice and steady, Mr. Jenkins," the captain said from behind me. "That's what I want on this watch. Nothing fancy, and no surprises."

"Aye, sir," I said. "No surprises."

The first couple of hours went just as the captain had requested, nothing fancy and no surprises. Alex was monitoring her board closely, keeping a comm channel open down to Cartography to make sure they were receiving the full data set from her sensors.

I was thinking about lunch, and enjoying watching Alex work, when I saw her stiffen in her seat. Instantly I was alert once more, daydreams and my aching muscles forgotten.

"Sir," she said, and I could hear the tension in her voice, "I'm picking up an anomaly on the hyperwave."

I frowned, thinking about what she'd just said. The hyperwave detection grid detected disturbances in hyperspace. These disturbances were most commonly caused by gravity sources, which showed up as holes in the grid. The stronger the gravity well, the larger the hole. But moving ships also showed up as holes; the bigger the ship, or the faster it was moving, the larger the hole in the grid. An anomaly meant she'd picked up a gravity source in what should have been empty space.

"Lovejoy," the captain said. I understood what he meant, and I agreed with him completely. I rose from my seat and turned my board over to the lieutenant. Captain Browne didn't say anything else to me, so I remained where I was, watching how Lt. Lovejoy handled the controls.

"What have we got, Ensign?" the captain asked.

Alex shrugged, keeping her attention on her readouts. "It's too early to say, sir," she said. "The signal is at the extreme edge of the grid," she rattled off some coordinates that put it well ahead of us and slightly to starboard. "I'm only picking up the outer edge of its gravity well. Extrapolating from that, I'd put this source's equivalent mass to that of a small planet, and its apparent motion is zero, sir."

Its apparent motion was zero, I thought. That meant it was not moving relative to the other objects in this region. In practical terms, it was standing still, which ruled out a number of things.

"Confirm that reading, Ensign," the captain said.

Alex's hands flew across her board, calibrating and adjusting her controls. "Reading confirmed, sir."

"Hmmm." I looked back at the captain. He stood motionless, his hands clasped behind his back, a thoughtful look on his face. "It's the size of a small planet, it's not moving, and it's in a place where, according to our charts, no planet exists. Speculations, Ensign?"

"It can't be a rogue dwarf or a black hole," Alex replied, keeping her attention on her board. "Either of those would be moving through this sector, not drifting along, which means it's probably not a natural phenomenon, but it's too massive to be a ship. To register this much mass, even our biggest ship of the line would have to be travelling very fast, but this signal is not moving. Which only leaves two possibilities that I can see, sir: a cluster of ships so close together that from this distance they read as a single source, or a very large, very dense space station."

I tensed, sudden excitement coursing through me. I could feel a similar tension in the atmosphere of the bridge. What she was describing could only be one thing, the one thing the Space Guard had been seeking for years: a hidden base far enough off the regular shipping lanes to avoid detection, yet close enough to strike virtually anywhere.

No one said it out loud, not even Alex, but I could tell that everyone on that bridge was thinking the same thing. Alex had just described what could only be the pirates' home base.

"Ensign Bailey," the captain said. Jonathan Bailey was the first shift communications officer. He'd trained me during my first week on board, but we hadn't spoken much since. He was a nice enough guy, and we'd gotten along all right, but we didn't have much in common and weren't likely to become good friends. "Send a 'heads up' to Command, but be circumspect. Alert them that we have an anomaly here. Include a live feed from Ensign McMichaels' scanners, but omit any speculation."

"Aye, sir," Bailey said, his hands flying across his panel, changing settings and splicing the scanner feed into his board. "Message away," he said moments later.

The captain nodded. "All right, Mr. Lovejoy. Take us in, straightline."

It never occurred to me to wonder why we were heading in to investigate rather than running away. We were a Guard ship, for one thing, which meant that it was our duty to investigate anomalies like this one. Even more importantly, however, if that *was* the pirates' headquarters we had stumbled across, we had to take advantage of our good fortune. If we waited for reinforcements, there was every chance that the pirates would simply pack up and move, and be gone before help could arrive.

No, I wasn't surprised that the captain ordered us to proceed, but his very last word did surprise me. "Straightline" meant going in toward your target in a direct line, taking no evasive maneuvers whatsoever. But as I thought about it my surprise faded. The *Michelangelo* was a good sized ship, and we'd been moving at maximum speed through hyperspace—when travelling from system to system, virtually all ships always travelled at maximum speed. Unless you were a pirate, or a Guard ship on patrol, there simply wasn't any reason to go any slower. In this case, that meant that we would have made a fairly large blip on any hyperwave detectors in the area. If that was the pirates' home base, they'd be on the lookout for ships in the area—in fact, they'd probably have scanner units scattered around for several light minutes, increasing their effective detection range—and they would have certainly seen us already. Which meant that the captain was right. Subtlety would be wasted right now.

"Straightline, sir, aye," said Lt. Lovejoy.

I watched the calm, competent way that he took the new course from Jamie and brought us around to match it. His movements were smooth and efficient, and the big ship responded softly to his touch.

I wished then that I was back at Communications. I was glad that Lovejoy was in the pilot's chair—his experience was definitely needed right now—but I would have given a lot right then to have something to do. Standing there helplessly, with nothing to occupy my mind or my hands, was not the way I wanted to go into my first combat situation.

Jamie was busy, his eyes darting across his read-outs. Alex was fully occupied, straining her equipment for every bit of new information she could pass on to the captain. Even Ensign Bailey was concentrating on keeping the sensor feed flowing through his board and out to Command Central. It would take weeks for them to receive our message, even though he was using the hyperwave comm system, but at least if anything happened to us they would know as much as possible about what we had stumbled across.

We came in fast, Alex calling out data as her scanners, still locked in passive mode, picked up more and more information: EMF activity, radiation levels, reflectivity, mass and density readings, and a score of other variables. Some of what her scanners picked up came from the object itself. Much of the rest of the information came from an analysis of how it impacted on the fabric of space. And some came from studying how the thinly scattered hydrogen atoms in the surrounding space interacted with it. By routing her signal through Spectrography, she would also be able to report on the composition of the object out there.

I listened to her voice—calm, steady, professional—

and watched Lovejoy's hands. At the moment that he brought us out of hyperspace I shifted my attention to the forward viewscreen.

I'd expected something large. She'd described it as having the mass of a small planet, but we'd already decided that it couldn't be that. So I figured that this, whatever it was, would be enormous.

It wasn't.

I looked up at the screen and gasped, and so did about half the people on the bridge. As we'd expected, what lay before us wasn't a black hole or a rogue star, but it wasn't any well-hidden pirate space station, either.

No, what we were looking at was a ship, larger than the *Michelangelo* but still far too small for the readings we'd gotten. What was more, one glance was enough to tell us all the same thing: this ship had not been built by humans.

It had finally happened. After three centuries in space, mankind had its first solid evidence that we were not alone.

Chapter Eleven

The ship was cylindrical, and seemed to be assembled in pieces. It was made up of a series of five canister-shaped sections linked with short, round tubes. The two on the ends—fore and aft, I guessed, though which was which I couldn't tell—tapered to a point, and each section looked to be about the size of the *Michelangelo* herself. The hull itself was completely black, and utterly unmarked. If there was any writing on the ship, it was either on the far side or invisible to our scanners. The only thing we could detect was a row of what appeared to be five hatches that ran along the alien ship. From this distance, we could make out that they were perfectly round, but not whether they were open or closed.

Captain Browne was the first one to speak. I expected something momentous from him, something that would go down in history alongside Neil Armstrong's " . . . small step for man . . ." speech when he stepped out onto the surface of the moon, or Joan Hansen's " . . . wild and crazy ride . . ." comment when she became the first human ever to enter hyperspace. I expected something like that from Captain Browne. I figured every Space Guard captain had prepared a little speech to recite if it turned out to be their ship that first made contact.

I was disappointed. What he said was, "McMichaels, give me some details, dammit! What the hell *is* that thing?"

I couldn't help grinning just a little. Alex, at least, had gotten a bit of immortality. Her name would go down in history as the first word spoken after mankind made contact with an alien race.

Alex's hands were already flying across her board, and had been since before Lovejoy brought us out of hyper. "Passives aren't telling me much, sir," she said. Rules of Engagement dictated passives only when approaching a bogey. Only under direct order from the captain could she go to active sensors. "Mass readings we already know. I'm getting no signs of power generation, and spectrography indicates its heat signature matches the ambient temperature for this area. Visuals show a random pattern of pitting all along the hull, sir, consistent with damage from micro-meteorites. In short, sir, based on what the passives are telling me, I'd guess she's a derelict."

That didn't surprise me, though it was more than a little disappointing. It only made sense that it would be a derelict. The ship hadn't reacted to us at all, and it had to have come from a long way away. This wasn't a heavily travelled sector, but we had settled systems in virtually every direction, which meant that this ship had originated far beyond those systems . . . or else it had been here long before we ever reached this region of space.

"Ping it, Ensign," the captain said.

"Going to actives, aye," Alex responded. Her hands moved, and then a moment later they moved again, pressing the same controls. "Negative, sir," she said. "I'm getting no reading whatsoever. That hull must be absorbing the signal."

I hadn't thought that was possible, especially with no power output.

"Hmm," the captain said. "So your anomaly is keeping

secrets, eh, Ensign? I don't like that. Mr. Lovejoy, reverse course and back us off slowly. I want some separation between us. Take us out to a distance of twenty-five thousand kilometers."

"Aye, sir."

As Lovejoy backed us off, Alex compensated, magnifying the image in our viewer so that it stayed at a constant size.

"Ensign McMichaels, you have this shuttle rotation, don't you?"

"I do, sir," Alex said.

I got a sinking feeling at that. I paid some attention to the shuttle rotation, hoping one day to see my name on the list of pilots scheduled to fly one of the *Michelangelo*'s runabouts on a scouting mission, and I knew that Alex was listed as primary shuttle pilot for this rotation.

"Ensign Bailey, please summon Lt. Evans to the bridge, and ask the executive officer to take a team to the shuttle bay."

My sinking feeling got worse. Douglas Evans was the second watch scanner operator.

"Ensign McMichaels," the captain went on, "when Lt. Evans reports in, you will turn your board over to him and report to your shuttle. Full gear, Ensign. Lieutenant Commander Murdoch will captain the shuttle, but I'll expect you to bring everyone home safely."

"Aye, sir," she said. Richard Murdoch was the executive officer on board the *Michelangelo*, second only to Captain Browne himself, and full gear meant full survival gear: environmental suit, rations pack, and blaster.

My sinking feeling hit rock bottom. They were going to board the derelict, and Alex was going to fly them there.

The next ten minutes or so went by in a blur. Lt. Evans showed up, paused for a moment to stare at the image on our screen, and then took Alex's place at the scanner controls. Moments later she was gone, and three minutes after that Ensign Bailey confirmed that she had reported in from her shuttle, and that Mr. Murdoch had arrived with his boarding party. Five minutes after that, the shuttle, the *Michelangelo One*, was under power and under way.

I would have given almost anything to be on that ship with the boarding party, but I knew better than to even ask. Jamie and I were both raw recruits. We were lucky to be serving watches on the bridge. There was no way the captain was going to allow us to be part of something like this.

Alex had fed her scanner output directly to Lt. Evans's board. Lt. Evans, in turn, was patching Alex's signal to Ensign Bailey, who was routing it through his hyperwave communicator and sending it on to Command Central.

"Keep your distance, Ensign," Captain Browne said. "I want to see the far side of this ship, but I don't want you to approach within one thousand kilometers, is that understood?"

"One thousand klicks, aye, sir." Alex's voice was calm and professional, but I couldn't help wondering what emotions were churning within her. Fear? Excitement? Both? Or something else, some sort of emotion that I couldn't even begin to guess at.

"Lt. Evans, give me a split screen on our forward viewer," the captain said. "I want a realtime image from our perspective on the left, and the visual feed from the *Michelangelo One* on the right."

The feed from the shuttle was unmagnified, and the alien ship was lost against the sea of stars. It was big, easily four times the size of the *Michelangelo*, but not so big that it could be seen from this distance.

The backdrop of stars began to shift as Alex eased the shuttle to starboard. Without really thinking about it, I'd expected her to simply circle the ship, but she increased her ascension as she jetted away. She was going to give the captain a look at the topside and the underbelly of that ship, as well as its far side.

"*Michelangelo*, this is shuttle *One*. Commencing our run now."

The captain nodded, more to himself I thought than to anyone else. "Lt. Evans, I want to know if you pick up anything new, either on your scanners or on the feed from the shuttle."

"Aye, sir,"

"Ensign McMichaels," he went on, raising his voice slightly even though the comm unit would pick his words up just fine even if he whispered them, "keep it simple. Nothing fancy. If you see anything wrong, if you even get a bad feeling about this, I want you to turn that shuttle around and jet out of there. Is that understood?"

"Aye, captain." Alex's voice was still rock steady.

I stepped to my right to get a better look at the scanner board, being careful to keep out of the captain's line of sight. Lt. Evans had increased the magnification of the shuttle feed so that the image size was the same on both sides of the screen, but I wanted to be able to follow Alex as she brought her ship in. I could see that she was taking the captain's words to heart. She was still over fifteen hundred klicks out, and not closing rapidly at all. She was taking her time, allowing the alien ship to reveal its secrets slowly, and making sure to stay well back out of harm's way.

It took her twenty minutes to make one and a half revolutions of the alien ship and to take up a position on the far side, exactly one thousand kilometers out. She could have been there in half the time, but the captain was right, there was no need to hurry. That ship wasn't going anywhere. She could afford to take her time, and to back off if she had to.

Her sensors and viewers had picked up nothing new. We still hadn't seen anything resembling markings, though she did see three more rows of hatches, each row a quarter of the way around the hull. There was no sign of damage, nothing to indicate what had happened to it, or why it was there. We also hadn't seen anything that looked like portals or sensors or weapons. Except for the hatches and the random pitting from micro-meteorites, the hull was smooth and unmarked.

"Ping it, Ensign," Captain Browne said when she was in position.

"Going to actives, aye, sir."

My hands had grown sweaty and I wiped them along the legs of my jumpsuit as I kept my eyes glued to Evans's controls, watching for the first sign of trouble. There wasn't any, though. As before, the ship didn't respond, and Alex's signal did not return to her board.

"Negative, sir," Lt. Evans said. "No reading at all."

"Mr. Murdoch," the captain said. If he was disappointed or disturbed, I couldn't tell from his voice. He sounded as calm as if he discovered unresponsive alien ships every day. "How does it look to you?"

"She's quiet, sir," the XO said. I had met the ship's executive officer when I first came aboard the *Michelangelo*, but I had yet to serve a watch under him. He'd struck me as a typical officer, calm, quiet, and competent, but I didn't know much about him. "What's more, sir, the scanners aren't picking up anything new, but she's got that feeling to her. I think it's safe to approach."

I glanced back at the captain. His lips were pursed, but beyond that he hadn't reacted at all.

"Ensign McMichaels," he said, "you are cleared to approach the vessel. Do not approach to any closer than one hundred meters, and my earlier instructions still stand: at the first sign of activity, get my people out of there."

"Aye, sir."

The *Michelangelo One* moved in closer. As before, Alex didn't take her in straightline, but rather brought her in on a spiral approach, minimizing the speed of her approach but maximizing the surface area of the ship they could see.

Once in position, Alex put her shuttle into a search pattern, circling the alien ship from a hundred meters out, overlapping her orbits as though she were mapping its surface. And, I realized, that's exactly what she was doing, building overlapping scanner shots of the vessel. It took quite a while—she spent more than forty-five minutes at it—but no one on board either ship seemed in a hurry.

From a hundred meters out, the alien ship didn't look any different. With magnification, we still couldn't find any signs of markings, sensors, or weapons. We couldn't even identify anything that looked like an engine.

Lt. Evans reported the moment that Alex had completed her final pass. "Imaging complete, sir," he said.

The captain nodded. "Good. And tell me, Lt. Evans, did we learn anything?"

The scanner operator shook his head. "No, sir," he said. "Nothing we didn't already know."

Captain Browne frowned. "So we still don't even know if those round markings are hatches, or whether they're open or closed."

"That's correct, sir."

"Well," the captain said. "Let's find out. Mr. Murdoch, go to full actives. Ensign McMichaels, you are cleared to approach to within ten meters."

The shuttle lit up like a spotlight, and I understood what the captain meant by "full actives." Alex had turned on every piece of search equipment on board the *Michelangelo One*, including putting the modified pulse radar on constant ping and turning on the array of powerful searchlights mounted to the shuttle's hull. Those searchlights were designed to cycle through much of the spectrum, including infrared and ultraviolet. Spectrography would record her visuals and analyze the absorption spectrum given off by the ship.

Once again, Alex took her shuttle around the alien

vessel, bathing every inch of its surface with light. She spent more than an hour at it, and evoked no response whatsoever from the alien ship. At the end of that time we had learned exactly one thing: those dark circles were different from the rest of the ship, but we couldn't say how or why. They did not reflect light, at least not like the rest of the hull did. Shining the spots on them was like aiming a flashlight into a bottomless pit—there was nothing to see, just a blackness that seemed to go on forever.

"Speculations?" the captain asked. "Anyone?"

Jamie and I glanced at each other briefly, but neither of us said anything. I had nothing to contribute, and even if I did have any ideas I would have felt too intimidated to open my mouth.

Lt. Evans was the first to speak. "If the interior is completely light absorptive, we might see an image similar to this."

The captain nodded. "The light goes in, but it doesn't reflect back."

"Aye, sir. Just like our pings didn't reflect back from the hull."

That didn't make sense to me. Not that Lt. Evans was wrong—he wasn't; I imagined that a completely light absorptive surface would behave exactly as he described. But it didn't make sense. An outer hull that couldn't be picked up by radar made perfect sense, but who would paint the *inside* of their ship with something that would make it impossible for its occupants to see?

I had no sooner asked that question when the answer came from somewhere deep within me: *aliens*, I thought. This ship wasn't built by people who thought like we did, or maybe by people who didn't even see like we did. Maybe they were a race of psychics, and light merely distracted them. Or maybe they operated solely by feel, or by smell. Or—

I cut my imagination off. I got the point. I couldn't

judge the builders of that ship by what seemed logical to me. Instead, I had to look at the situation itself, and allow it to build its own logic.

One thing bothered me, though, as I thought about what Lt. Evans had said. I kept waiting for someone else to mention it, but no one did. They simply batted around other ideas which might explain what we were seeing within those hatches—light absorptive material bonded to the *outside* of the hatches, meaning that they were closed but they *looked* open, though no one could come up with even the most unlikely scenario to explain why anyone would want to do that; trans-dimensional warps that operated in one direction only, meaning that our light went into the hatch and was transported to some other dimension before it touched anything; and other, even less plausible ideas. The trans-dimensional warp idea was rejected because we assumed it would take power to maintain such a portal, and we weren't picking up any energy readings at all.

Which was when I spoke up. I didn't want to, but I just had to.

"Um, sir?" I said.

The captain looked over at me. "Yes, Jenkins?" he said. He took a closer look at me and smiled softly. "Don't be shy," he added. "You're on board because you're a Guardsman. You've earned the right to be heard."

Yeah, I thought. *An* apprentice *Guardsman*. And here I was about to shoot my mouth off to the captain himself. But I already knew I had no choice.

"There may be power readings after all, sir," I said. "If, for whatever reason, there *is* a material within that ship that absorbs light, it would also absorb much of what we use to detect energy output. It would absorb any infrared signatures given off by the heat of operating equipment. It would absorb the light from any dials or displays. It would absorb—"

The captain raised his hand, cutting me off. "Good

point," he said. "Let's think about this. If the inner hull of the *Michelangelo* was covered with a light absorptive material, we could still see each other. We could read all our instruments. We could, in short, perform all our regular duties—"

"—But no sign of any of this would escape the ship," Mr. Murdoch finished for him, his voice coming over the comm link with the shuttle. "Very clever—and good thinking, Mr. Jenkins."

I felt my face growing hot. Jamie winked and grinned at me, which didn't help any, but no one else paid me any attention.

"Recommendations, Mr. Murdoch?" the captain said.

The XO didn't hesitate. "I think we should board her, sir," he said. "It's obvious that we're not going to learn anything more from out here, and we have an obligation to explore further." The captain didn't say anything, and he added, "Request permission to board her, Captain."

The captain paused. He thought about it for nearly twenty seconds before replying. "Negative," he said. "Mr. Murdoch, what I want you to do is to take your boarding party and cross over to that vessel. I want all your people in full gear and tethered to each other and to the shuttle. You are authorized to make contact with the outer hull. You are authorized to attempt to take physical samples of the outer hull. You are expressly *not* authorized to make any effort to enter that ship. Is that understood, Mr. Murdoch?"

"Understood, sir. Thank you, sir."

He hadn't given Alex permission to approach any closer, so she left the shuttle where it was, exactly ten meters out from the alien ship. The airlock on the shuttle was on the far side from us, and the atmosphere on the bridge grew tense as we waited for the first sign of the boarding party.

We didn't have long to wait. Less than two minutes after the captain gave permission, we saw the first crewman emerge from behind the *Michelangelo One*. At first I couldn't tell who it was—I still didn't know all my shipmates, and I had no idea who Lt. Commander Murdoch had selected to accompany him. After a moment, though, I could see the gold insignia on the side of the helmet, and I knew it was Murdoch himself. Behind him, the other two boarders emerged from behind the shuttle. Together, the three formed an equilateral triangle about ten feet across and in line with the plane formed by our three ships.

I could picture Alex sitting at the controls, her helmet sealed up, breathing her suit's air. Her suit would be nothing like the ones we'd used on the *Hobo One*, our shuttle back on Brighthome. Those had been generic, all-purpose, one-size-fits-all emergency suits. Here in the Guard, everyone had custom-fitted light blue suits, with Space Guard patches on the left shoulder and insignia worn on the side of the helmet and over the left breast.

Jamie and I had even been issued our own suits. The only time we'd worn them was when we tried them on for size, and I was looking forward to wearing off that new suit smell. For that matter, I was just looking forward to my first trip out into space itself, away from the ship. I had never done that—at least as far back as I could remember—and I wanted to.

The boarding party moved away from the shuttle, powered by the small jet packs each one wore. Those were standard Guard issue, with both pressurized gas tanks and a small chemical reaction motor mounted to them. For most work, the pressurized gas was enough to move slowly through space, but the more powerful thruster was there for emergencies. As they neared the derelict itself, I could see the thin, strong cables linked between them and connecting each of them to the shuttle.

The two Guardsmen in the rear fired their jets simultaneously, killing their forward momentum and coming to a stop halfway between the shuttle and the alien ship. The lieutenant commander continued forward, three thin tethers stretching out behind him. Everyone on the bridge held their breath as he neared the craft.

Lt. Commander Murdoch killed his own momentum and halted next to the ship. Slowly he reached out and laid his gloved hand on the smooth, black alien surface.

Nothing happened, and we all started breathing normally again.

"She's real, Captain." The lieutenant commander's voice came over the comm channel.

Captain Browne chuckled. "Very good, Mr. Murdoch. Proceed."

He brought his boots into contact with the ship, but it was obvious that their magnetized soles couldn't find any purchase.

"I can't walk on her, sir," he reported in. "There's no discernible gravity, and the hull is non-magnetic."

Which was odd, I thought. It had shown up on the hyperwave detection grid as having the mass of a small planet, and yet there was no discernible gravity. No one else mentioned it, however, so I kept my mouth shut and focussed on the captain's response.

"Inform your team to use their jets, Mr. Murdoch," the captain said, "but be careful. I don't want someone accidentally swinging their legs into a hatch."

"Aye, sir."

The captain could have passed the order on himself, of course. The entire boarding party, and Alex herself, was hearing everything that was said on that channel, but protocol required a chain of command. I knew the captain well enough by now to know that he would only break protocol in an emergency.

It was fascinating watching the boarding party at work. I'd seen simulations of this, both in the Space Guard vids I used to watch back on Brighthome and in some of the training sessions I'd had here on the *Michelangelo*, but this was the first time I'd been able to observe the real thing, as it happened.

The three of them worked as a unit. Each of them always seemed to know where the other two were, and they instinctively worked to keep their lines clear. That was made easier by the smoothness of the hull—there was nothing sticking up to interfere with their tethers—but I could tell that it didn't make any real difference. They were also careful to make sure that none of their lines got too close to one of those mysterious black hatches.

Their physical examination didn't take long. The ship didn't react to their presence, and there was nothing on the outer hull for them to examine. They were able to take scratchings from each section, and then the lieutenant commander went over to examine one of the hatches himself.

On the bridge, we had two different views of Murdoch bringing his faceplate close to the surface of the ship, examining the hatch from every angle.

After a few moments, he reported in, "Nothing, Captain. There's no sign of a seal, nothing to indicate there's anything here. I can't see anything inside at all—not the edge of the hull, nothing. It's like the outer skin of this vessel just . . . disappears."

The captain nodded, though I was sure he didn't have a clue what that meant, any more than the rest of us did. "Proceed, Mr. Murdoch," he said, his voice carefully calm and neutral.

One of the crewmen briefly crossed back to the shuttle to deliver the samples to Alex and then rejoined the other two at the alien ship. He brought back a remote unit, a small, radio-controlled probe that was capable of taking visual readings across a large section of the spectrum and could perform a few other limited tasks. It was designed for use in space, most commonly in ships that had been boarded by the pirates and left to adrift. Its most common use was to check for booby traps and for survivors. I'd often wondered if it was just such a device that had first found me, alone and adrift in that survival pod.

"We've done all we can here, Captain," Mr. Murdoch reported in as the third crewman joined him with the remote unit. "Request permission to send in the eye, sir."

The captain hesitated, which surprised me. To this point, both he and the lieutenant commander had been very methodical, going through the motions, being very cautious, but it had been obvious from the very beginning that if we were going to learn anything new, someone— or something—was going to have to enter that ship. I didn't understand why the captain was hesitating now that the moment was upon us. Of course, I also realized that I didn't have the responsibility for these men's lives on my shoulders.

"Lt. Evans," the captain said. "Activate the feed from the eye and put it on the forward viewer. I want our own realtime image in the top left, the feed from the shuttle in the top right, and the image from the eye on the bottom."

Lt. Evans was almost as fast carrying out the orders as the captain was giving them.

"Mr. Murdoch," the captain went on. "You have control of the eye. Proceed."

The third crewman handed the control unit to the lieutenant commander.

"Proceeding, aye, sir."

Mr. Murdoch powered up the eye. It had three powerful spotlights built along its underside, one forward, one aft, and one in the middle, as well as one on its dorsal side in the middle. All four lights came on, and the bottom half of our forward viewscreen came alive.

Mr. Murdoch gave the eye a quick test, powering forward and backwards, turning it left and right and up and down, and swivelling each of the lights.

"She checks out, sir," he said. "Beginning our approach now."

The captain stayed silent as the lieutenant commander brought the remote unit closer to the nearest hatch. He was at the middle section of the alien ship. I didn't know if that was by design or if he just happened to be there, but that was the section he chose to explore first. The other two crewmen were close by, their tethers taut, ten feet away and motionless. None of the three was in direct contact with the ship, but all were close enough to reach out and touch it if they wanted to.

Lt. Evans kept his eyes on his board. Everyone else kept theirs glued to the forward screen. I did, too, though I couldn't help looking around at my shipmates briefly, sharing in this exciting and wonderful moment.

The black hole of the hatch grew larger on the viewscreen. Once again, the air on the bridge became close and heavy as we all held our breath.

Mr. Murdoch started a countdown as the remote unit came even closer. "Contact in three, two, one—"

His voice cut off. At the moment the eye penetrated the outer hull, the alien ship disappeared, utterly and completely and without any warning whatsoever.

And that wasn't all. The remote unit, and all three of the crewmen who had hung in space near the ship had all vanished as well. The *Michelangelo* herself and her shuttle were left, just two ships and a whole galaxy full of unanswered questions.

Chapter Twelve

The captain reacted immediately. "Evans, McMichaels, report! What the hell happened?" On screen, the feed from the eye had gone silent. The bottom half of the viewer was just empty. Above it, we saw a view of the shuttle on the left, three empty tethers stretching away, and the signal from the shuttle showed us the *Michelangelo* herself. But the alien ship was nowhere in sight.

Lt. Evans sagged back in his seat, his hands slipping from his board. "It's—it's gone, sir."

Alex had little more to offer. "I don't know, sir," she said. "There were no indications of power buildup, no sign of movement, and spectrographic analysis does not reveal the presence of any sort of field surrounding the ship just before it vanished. Safety lines appear to have been cut. We'll know more after we examine their ends and take exact measurements."

The captain was frowning, his hands clasped at his sides. "Are we getting any readings from the boarding party at all? Radio feed, telemetry data, anything?"

Lt. Evans shook his head. "Negative, sir, and the hyperwave is empty as well. She's just gone, sir, and she's taken them with her."

The captain's shoulders slumped briefly, and I could only imagine what he was feeling. He'd been in the Guard long enough that he'd probably sent crewmen to their deaths before, in battle against the pirates, in dangerous rescue missions, and even on new world explorations, but this had to be harder than any of those. There was no logic here, no rational explanation to take comfort in, and, worst of all, no lesson to be learned. The captain had done nothing wrong, and yet three crewmen were lost.

"Ensign McMichaels," he said, his voice carrying only a hint of his pain, "bring the shuttle home. There's nothing more for you to do out there."

"But, sir—"

I was astonished to hear Alex arguing. And by the looks on their faces, so was everyone else on the bridge.

"That's an order, Ensign. Bring her home."

Alex paused, then acknowledged the order. "Aye, sir," she said, but I could hear the reluctance in her voice. "*Michelangelo One* coming home."

"Mr. Bailey, end the signal to Command. Conclude it with a request for assistance and advice."

"Ending signal, aye, sir."

Nothing fancy, the captain had said when I took the helm. No surprises. I wished now that I had been able to give him what he'd asked for. Our moment of glory, mankind's first contact with the relic of an alien civilization, had turned to utter defeat. We felt as if we had just lost a war, one that we hadn't even known we'd been fighting.

"New standing orders, Mr. Bailey. Log them and inform Command. The *Michelangelo* will remain on station here until we learn what happened to that ship and our missing crewmen, until their stores are all used up and there is no hope whatsoever, or until we receive a direct order from Command to move on. Is that clear, Ensign Bailey?"

"Very clear, sir."

"Good. As of now, I want everyone on board working overtime on this problem: what happened to that ship? Where could it have gone? I want theories, observations, speculations, crazy ideas, anything that might shed some light on this. This is not classified, but it *is* top priority. Make sure the full data sets from all logs and sensors are available to everyone."

A chorus of "ayes" answered him.

Jamie and I glanced at each other. I could see in his eyes all the same emotions that were churning within me, and a silent communication passed between us. I had no idea what we could do, what the two of us had to offer, but we were going to do everything we could to help out. We weren't just passengers on this ship, we were Guardsmen, and we were determined to find a way to make a difference.

The rest of the watch passed in a sort of stunned silence. Orders were given in soft tones, and there was almost no chatter or conversation at all. Alex reported back to the bridge after dressing down her shuttle, but she didn't have anything to add to her report. Lt. Evans turned his board back over to her, but requested and received permission to stay on the bridge.

There was nothing anyone could do, but none of us wanted to leave. Slowly, however, watches came to an end, and the captain started ordering people to stand down. Jamie was the first to leave, followed by Alex and Ensign Bailey. My turn came later, long after the captain himself should have been relieved. He made no move to leave his station, however, and I didn't blame him a bit. I would have stayed, too, if there had been anything for me to do, any way for me to feel useful.

I saluted the captain before I left, something we rarely did, but it seemed called for somehow. He didn't return the salute, but he did give me a brief smile before returning his attention to the forward viewscreen.

I looked once more at that empty, desolate field of stars, and then I headed below to find food, Jamie, and Alex. We had work to do.

Chapter Thirteen

I found Alex almost by accident. I was looking for her, but she wasn't in any of the places I'd expected. I stopped by her quarters—she had a small wardroom she shared with Ensign Maya Malone—but there was no sign of her. I went to our assigned mess hall and grabbed a quick bite, but she wasn't there, either. I stopped by the gym, thinking she might be working out her fear and her anger, but the place was empty. I looked into Cartography, on the off chance that she was burying herself in her work, and I even checked the library in case she was pouring over the sensor records of the alien ship, but she was in none of those places.

She was in the lounge, the one place I'd never seen her, and she had a glass of something dark and cold in front of her. She wasn't drinking it, though. She was merely staring down into it, her hands curled around the glass, a lost look on her face.

"Alex," I said, slipping into the seat across from her. She didn't react at all to my presence, but that didn't bother me. She looked so hurt, so confused, and I reached out and touched her hands.

She moved, then, straightening in her seat and pulling

her hands away. Her eyes slowly swivelled to meet mine, and the pain I saw in them was sharp and intense.

"It's my fault," she said, her voice a broken husk of what it had been.

"Don't be silly," I said, but she shook her head, her eyes flashing with sudden anger.

"I was the pilot," she said. "Mr. Murdoch was in charge, but I was the pilot. The safety of the crew was my responsibility, and I failed. It was my fault, Tom."

I longed to reach for her again, but I didn't. I kept my hands still on the table. "There was nothing you could have done—"

"What do you know about it, Tom?" she demanded. "What do you know about having the lives of other people in your hands? About letting them down, seeing them die?"

Her words cut me like a knife, and she wasn't through yet. Pushing her chair back, she stood and looked down at me. "You fly some combat missions, Tom. You watch your friends and your crewmates fall under enemy fire. You feel what it's like to be the sole survivor, and then you come talk to me."

I understood what was happening, of course. She'd probably sat there since she got off watch, not drinking necessarily but brooding, her anger, her fear, her frustrations, and her worry all churning around within her, looking for a target. She didn't really mean what she was saying. She was just venting.

I understood that, but dissecting her words didn't take away their sting.

She didn't wait for me to answer. She just picked up her glass, drained it, and then stalked out of the bar, leaving me to sit in silence.

I watched her leave. When she'd gone, when she could no longer hear me, I answered her, softly, hearing the pain in my own voice. "I have, Alex," I said, my voice barely above a whisper. I thought about that survival pod they'd found me in, and I wondered yet again what it had meant, who I had been, what had happened, and I thought I could understand something of what she was feeling. "I have," I said again, "and it wasn't your fault."

I glanced once at the bar itself with its automated drink dispenser, and then I rose and walked away. There were no answers there, and no consolation, either.

Jamie was in our wardroom, but he wasn't playing one of his vids. He was using the computer console, working on something that looked like some kind of diagram or schematics.

"Hey, buddy," I said.

He was caught up in whatever it was he was working on and barely glanced at me. At least, I hoped that was the reason. He'd been pretty cool toward me since I'd left him to eat with the lieutenants, but I was convinced that was merely coincidence. He'd been busy, and we just hadn't had time to get together.

"What are you working on?" I asked.

"Sensor reduction analysis," he said, not taking his eyes off his screen.

"Oh," I said.

He paused then and looked at me, a slow grin spreading across his face. He knew that I didn't have a clue what "sensor reduction analysis" meant.

"I'm looking at the software that reduces the input from the scanners into manageable chunks and then analyzes them. I want to see if there's a way to improve performance enough to learn something—anything—about that ship."

"Oh," I said again. I wanted to add, "Can I help?" but I didn't bother. I could do a lot of things, but computers were Jamie's area, and I could help him the most by simply staying out of his way. "Good idea. You want me to bring you something from the mess hall?"

He shook his head. "I ate, thanks. Just make sure I don't sleep through my next watch."

He had a habit of getting engrossed in these puzzles and staying up really late working on them. Back on Brighthome, I'd often had to drag him out of bed in time for his morning classes.

"You got it," I said.

He grinned and nodded, but already I could see that his thoughts were turning back to his project.

"Well, let me know if there's anything I can do to help."

Jamie sort of grunted at me, acknowledging what I'd said without really hearing it. I grinned, but there was a touch of bitterness to my humor. Such dreams I'd had—still had, for that matter. Dreams of making a difference, of being involved, of doing good. Yet here I was, caught up in the biggest discovery since hyperspace, and there was nothing I could do. I couldn't help Jamie with his programming. I couldn't help our missing crewmen. I couldn't even help Alex deal with her anger and her pain.

Back on Brighthome, I used to head to the caves when I got to feeling this way. Here on board the *Michelangelo*, I had the old war room I'd found, but that was too small, too cramped for what I needed. I wanted distraction. I wanted people. But most of all I wanted something to do.

Feeling utterly useless, I turned and headed out to roam the ship.

Chapter Fourteen

I had nothing to do, and nowhere in particular to go, so I just explored the ship. I started at the top, up near the bridge, wandering through officer country. I would have liked to wander onto the bridge itself, just to see if anything new had happened, but I knew better. The bridge was no place for sightseeing.

The closed doors of officer country drew my eyes as I walked through the corridors. I liked to daydream, to envision a day when I had a rank above Apprentice Guardsman, when I had the right to wear gold on my shoulders and to walk through those doors. It might never happen, but now that one dream of mine had come true I knew that I would never stop dreaming again.

I thought about the alien ship as I roamed, wondering how long it had been drifting there, wondering why it had chosen that particular moment to come to life, wondering where it had gone and what technology had taken it away so fast.

So many questions, and I didn't have even the faintest beginnings of an answer.

One thing was obvious, though: it was no coincidence

that the ship disappeared when it did. We'd picked up no energy readings whatsoever from the derelict ship, but somehow it had been able to sense the moment that its hatch was breached—and not only sense it, it had been able to react to that breach in a way we didn't yet understand.

But where had it gone? And how? And why?

And, most importantly, could we find a way to go there, too?

There was a word that had disappeared from the conversations on board the *Michelangelo*. The crew was quieter than normal anyway, subdued by the shock and the suddenness of what had happened. But as I roamed the ship, listening in on the fragments of conversation I picked up in the corridors, I noticed there was one word that had to be on everyone's mind, but that no one was saying, and that word was time.

The boarding party had taken extra rations. With the recyclers in their suits, and with the supplies they had with them, they had enough food and water to last for two weeks. They had also taken along extra oxygen bottles, and with a reclamation rate of over ninety-five percent, they would have enough air to last them for a few days after their other supplies ran out.

But that was if everything went exactly as planned, and if the boarding party went into virtual hibernation. They'd have to lower the heat on their suits, stop moving, and slow their metabolic systems down. In short, they'd have to decide to wait for us to come to them, and none of that was likely to happen.

First and foremost, they had to know that something had happened, and while they were too well trained to panic, still their systems were going to react to the new stress levels. Their metabolic rates would go up, not down, as their bodies instinctively tried to provide them with the resources to deal with what had happened. Also, we had to assume that the boarding party would not

simply settle in, conserving their resources and waiting
for us to find them. Instead, they would be actively
exploring the alien ship, trying to understand its workings
enough to figure out how to bring it back from wherever
it had gone. We had to assume that—and we also had
to hope that. As much of a long shot as it was, they still
had better odds of figuring out an utterly alien technology
than we had of finding them in time. Given a year or
two to explore, and a squadron of our fastest ships,
maybe we'd have a chance. But we didn't have a year
or two. We had less than two weeks, and the *Michelangelo* was on her own.

That was the situation as I saw it, and though no one
on board was talking about it where I could hear, I was
pretty sure that I had it right. There just weren't that
many options. So, assuming the boarding party was still
alive and still able to function, we had to expect that they
were going to work as hard and as long as they could
to get home. Which meant that they should have enough
food, water, and air to survive ten days or so.

That was our deadline. Not ten days to figure out what
had happened, but ten days to figure out what had
happened, how to solve it, and then to do it. Because
the odds were good that if we found our missing crewmates eleven days from now, it would be a day too late.

I looked once more at the closed doors leading to the
various officers' quarters, and for once I was glad that
I didn't have a place among them yet. There was a load
of responsibility that came with those gold bars, and at
times that load could simply be too heavy to bear.

I thought about Captain Browne, and the load he was
carrying right now, and I didn't envy him his position
at all.

Thinking such thoughts, I found the closest ladder and
went below decks, down to more familiar levels, down
to where I belonged.

Chapter Fifteen

I ran into Maya Malone near the cafeteria. Maya and I were never going to be great friends. She was Alex's bunkmate, and I was pretty sure she had a good idea how I felt about Alex—and I was even more sure that she didn't approve.

Ensign Malone was a combat specialist. She could field strip a blaster faster than I could find a target to shoot at and spent most of her watches as a gunnery officer. I suspected that she had been disappointed with the role the *Michelangelo* had played against the pirates when Old Jack was captured—she would have wanted to be on the front lines, not playing deep support—and I think she held that against me.

Or maybe she just didn't like me.

She was cute, though, a little shorter than Alex, with blonde hair and blue eyes and an iron-hard handshake. I'd once toyed with the idea of double dating, me with Alex, Maya with Jamie, but that was never going to happen. For that matter, I was beginning to believe that Alex and I were never going to happen.

"Ensign Malone," I said, nodding to her politely. I

intended to step around her and keep walking but she put up a hand.

"Tom," she said. "I've been looking for you."

That surprised me. It also made me worried. I didn't think that Maya had suddenly come to her senses and decided that Alex and I were the perfect match. More likely she had come to deliver some sort of stern warning to me.

"Yes?" I said, my voice guarded.

If she heard the stiffness in my voice, she gave no sign of it. "I'm worried about Alex," she said. "You know what happened earlier, don't you?"

I nodded. "I was on the bridge," I said.

She gave me a sharp, hard look, and for a moment I didn't understand why, and then it occurred to me: Maya was jealous of me. It made sense, sort of. I mean, here I was, less than four weeks on board, holding only the honorary rank of Apprentice Guardsman, still months away from being able to officially join the Guard, and yet I was serving watches on the bridge and even piloting the *Michelangelo* herself. I could see where Maya might not understand all that—I didn't truly understand it myself. But the thought that she might be jealous of me, that was a new one.

"Yeah," she said, dismissing my comment, "well, then you know that Alex was piloting the shuttle, and you know Alex. She takes her responsibilities very seriously."

"She's blaming herself," I said.

"Of course. Wouldn't you?"

"But it wasn't her fault," I said. "There was nothing she could have done."

"Tell her that," Maya said. "I'm not a pilot. It doesn't mean as much coming from me. But you've earned your flames. It might mean something from you."

I looked away, staring off toward the grey bulkhead but seeing the scene in the bar earlier. "I did," I said in a soft voice. "It didn't help."

Maya stiffened beside me, and I could feel her withdrawing from me. For a moment there we'd had the chance to heal some of the rift between us, a rift that centered around Alex, and that might have been healed for her sake. But that moment was gone. Maya had come to me for help, and there was nothing I could do.

"Well," she said, "thanks for trying." But there was no warmth in her voice, no sincerity. Which was just as well. I wasn't pleased with my efforts, either.

She hesitated a moment as though waiting for me to say something, or perhaps she was trying to think of something else to say herself, but then she just turned and walked away without another word.

I watched her go, and I was surprised at the sudden emptiness I felt inside. Another chance missed, another opportunity that had slipped past. There had been too many of those lately. Joining the Guard was supposed to be my dream come true—and there had been some wonderful things happen since I came on board. It was just that there had been some less-than-wonderful things happen, too, and I was beginning to believe that those things were the more important ones.

Shaking my head, I made an effort to pull myself out of the blue funk that had descended on me. It was time for a workout, and I was ready, even if it would be Will Davies and not Alex who worked with me.

Putting Maya and Alex out of my thoughts, I found the nearest ladder and headed for the gym.

Chapter Sixteen

I put everything I had into the punch, all my anger, all my frustration, all my built-up loneliness and hurt and despair. It helped that I was throwing it at Ensign Davies, who was the cause of some of those feelings. I started it from my hip, just as Alex had shown me, driving the blow forward, going for both speed and power.

My fist snapped out and it felt like a good strike. He had left himself open just the tiniest bit, overextending slightly on a roundhouse kick that had missed, and I had visions of seeing my blow land solidly on Davies' face. In my mind, I could already feel the impact of his cheekbone against my knuckles. I knew I shouldn't enjoy this, and that I should pull my punch, but I just couldn't help myself.

At the last moment, Will leaned slightly to his left, his right hand coming up and touching the outside of my wrist. It looked like a simple brush, but it deflected my fist to the side of his face. In the next moment, his hand was streaking toward me, not so much a second motion as a continuation of his block, only now it had become an attack, fast and hard and unerringly accurate.

He was nicer than me. He pulled his punch, stopping

his fist with his knuckles just barely touching the end of my nose.

We held like that, motionless, my fist hanging in the air beside him, his hovering directly before me, for two beats of my pounding heart. Then he stepped back and lowered his hand.

"Not bad, Tom," he said. "You're getting better, but you've got to work on picking up both your speed and your power. You're still too tense. Your body works against itself. You need to relax, let your movements flow, don't force them so much."

I nodded. I understood what he meant, but I didn't know what I could do about it. Part of it was simply that I was trying too hard, that I found myself with the chance to strike back at this guy who had caused me so much pain, and I just couldn't help it. It was too bad, too. Davies was actually a pretty nice guy—which I'd figured out already, of course. I hadn't expected that Alex would waste her time on a jerk. What's more, he seemed to be offering his friendship, and under other circumstances I would have been pleased to be his friend. But every time I tried to relax my mind offered up that image of Alex kissing him so softly in the hallway, and all my anger and pain came flooding back.

He bowed to me, signalling the end of our sparring. I returned the bow and as I did so I realized that there was nothing false about it. He was a good fighter, and an excellent teacher, and for that he had my respect. I just wished that was all there was to it.

As we walked over to where our towels were, I couldn't help asking him, "How's she doing?" I didn't have to say who "she" was. He knew who I meant.

He shrugged. "She's taking it pretty hard, as you'd expect."

He glanced over at me with an unreadable expression on his face, and I found myself wondering what he was thinking. How much had she told him about Brighthome?

Was it possible that he, of all people, occasionally felt jealous of me?

I tried not to smile, but that thought made me feel very good all of a sudden.

He shrugged again and nodded toward the entrance to the gym. "Here she is now." He shot me a half grin and added, "As for how she is, she asked me to work out with her today, and let's just say I don't expect her to be pulling her punches."

He left me then and went over to where she had started stretching. He took her in his arms and held her for a moment, but at least they didn't kiss and I could kid myself that it was only a friendly embrace. And maybe it was. Maybe he was just giving her the moral support that she needed right now.

They separated, bowed to each other, and started sparring, and I could see right away that he was right. I'd progressed to the point where I could actually follow most of the kicks and punches and blocks, and I could tell that she wasn't pulling her shots. He was blocking most of them, but a few of them were getting through, and they obviously hurt when they landed.

I watched for a few minutes and then I turned away. I wasn't sure why. I should have enjoyed seeing him take a pounding like that, but after only a few minutes I turned and headed over toward the punching bag.

As I turned away, I couldn't help wondering, could I do what he was doing? Even for Alex, could I stand there and let her pound on me without retaliating, without stepping up my own attacks?

I didn't know, and that bothered me more than anything else about that practice. I couldn't answer that question, and I should have been able to.

I started in on the bag, increasing the speed and power of my blows until I was putting everything I had into each one. Only it wasn't Will Davies' face I was seeing before me. It was my own.

Chapter Seventeen

Dinner was a lonely experience. Jamie was still up in our wardroom, buried in schematics and flow charts. I hadn't seen Alex since the gym. For all I knew, she was still there, still delivering blow after blow, punishing herself and everyone around her.

The mess hall was quiet. There was almost no conversation, and the little chatter I heard was hushed. The funny thing was that no one seemed to be talking about the alien ship or our missing crewmen. I couldn't tell if they were afraid of jinxing the situation, or if it was simply too painful to think about, much less talk about, and there was no one in the crew who I knew well enough to ask.

I ate quickly, paying no attention to my food. When it was gone, I put my tray away, but I wasn't ready to return to my bunk. I was tired from my workout, but I still had too much energy, too much restlessness, too many conflicting emotions bottled up within me and I just didn't know what to do with them.

I would have liked to go flying. If I'd been on Brighthome, I would have headed out to the caves, or taken my shuttle and gone exploring. But I wasn't on

Brighthome. I was on the Space Guard ship *Michelangelo*, with duties and responsibilities and a very limited range of distractions.

And that's what I needed right then: distraction. Something to take my mind off Alex, and the alien ship, and the missing crewmen, and my own growing feelings of loneliness and frustration.

Distraction. There was only one place on board the *Michelangelo* that I'd found that. Making up my mind, I took one last look around the mess hall and then headed for the ship's library.

The library was one of the few places on board where I felt truly at home. For all that this place was different from the library I'd grown used to on Brighthome, there were undeniable similarities, too. There were no books here, for example, and no librarian to help out. I wasn't sure which I missed more—the smell of paper and old leather or the friendly guidance of Mr. Murphy. But even with all its differences, there was a familiar feel to the place, and I felt my guards relax the moment I walked through the door.

I'd selected the farthest carrel from the door as my own personal workspace. As far as I knew, I could have used any of the six computer terminals, but this one called to me the first time I walked through the door, and it was the only one I used.

Grabbing a cup of coffee from the auto dispenser near the door, I headed over to my carrel. I didn't really like the stuff, but I was trying to acquire a taste for it. Everyone on board the *Michelangelo* drank it, and I wanted to fit in, not be different.

I took a sip of the dark, bitter liquid, made a face, and then set it beside the keyboard and forgot about it as I activated my workstation and called up a new search routine.

I had planned to resume my search for my past. That

was what I always did when I came here. It was a comfortable routine, something that I had made a part of my life here on the *Michelangelo*. I didn't truly expect to find anything—I'd given up on that particular dream back on Brighthome—but this was what I did. Jamie had his computers, Alex had her sensors, and I—well, I had my flames, but they didn't help me much now. After all, I couldn't exactly ask Captain Browne if I could borrow a shuttle for a few hours. Instead, I had my computers, and the search for my past that I had lost more than four years ago.

Sitting there in my carrel, staring at the screen, I saw the endless tree of possibilities stretching out before me, and in that moment the sheer impossibility of what I was attempting came home to me in a way it never had before. I mean, I had always known that this was a long shot. I had started doing this back on Brighthome out of boredom and a desperate need to find my past. Well, that need had faded with time, to the point where I could mostly accept that I would never know who I really was or where I came from, but still I came back to my search. Not out of boredom, not here on the *Michelangelo*, but out of habit, and, I guess, for the comfort that the familiar routine provided.

Now, however, it wasn't comfort that I was finding. We had crewmen lost in space; my friends were no longer talking to me; and I was feeling helpless and frustrated—and the last thing I needed was another failure to add to my list.

Leaning back in my chair, I ran my hands through my hair and made a face at the screen, glaring at it as though it was responsible for my feelings and my failings.

"All right," I said. "Figure it out. If you can't find yourself in these records, maybe you can find that alien ship."

I reached for my coffee, took a sip, and set it back down, thinking about what I had just said. Obviously, there wasn't going to be an entry marked "ALIEN SHIP—FOUND." No, if it was in the Guard's database, it would be under something more subtle than that.

I cleared the screen, saving my old search results to a file, and then, cracking my knuckles and stretching my neck to get the kinks out, I started playing with the records.

I lost myself in my search. My earlier work had all concentrated on missing person reports, and so I hadn't really explored the depth and breadth of the Space Guard's records. I was amazed by what I found. There were colonization records, star charts, spectrographic analyses of hundreds of systems, arrest records, firsthand accounts of various encounters with the pirates, and so much more. There were personnel files and case studies of the politics in different sectors. There were ships' histories and anecdotal accounts, manifests and inventories, communication logs and sensor reports, all filed and indexed and cross-referenced. Surely, I thought, somewhere in that ocean of data was the particular drop of information I was looking for.

I didn't find it. I spent an hour and a half searching, and though I learned a lot about the Guard and its history, I didn't find a single reference to anything that might have been the alien ship.

Picking up my now-cold coffee, I looked down into its black, oily depths and set it back down untouched. The stuff was bad enough piping hot.

Leaning back in my chair, I stretched my arms and back and neck and then powered down my terminal. I didn't bother saving any of my search results. I'd found stuff of interest, but nothing that would help us at all.

Rising, then, I took my cup to the recycler and dropped it in before heading back to my bunk. Maybe Jamie'd had more luck than I had, or maybe Captain Browne had thought of something.

I hoped so, anyway. If it was up to me to save our crewmen, they were in deep, deep trouble.

Chapter Eighteen

Jamie barely looked up when I walked into our wardroom. He was hunched over the workstation on the desk in the far corner, schematics and diagrams flashing by on the screen before him.

"How's it going, buddy?" I asked.

He grunted something unintelligible and kept looking at the screen.

For a moment I just stood there watching him, a taste like ashes in my mouth. If I could have, I'd have gone back in time to that moment in the cafeteria, and I'd have stayed with Jamie rather than going to eat with Lt. O'Malley.

But I couldn't. Like so many things lately, I was helpless to do anything more than watch.

Feeling frustration and bitterness welling up within me, I stripped off my jumpsuit and headed for the shower.

"I think it's a pirate trap."

Still feeling the sting of Jamie's rebuff, I had gone down to the mess hall for a light snack and had run into O'Malley, Wu, and Freeman. Now the four of us were

89

seated at a corner table, talking about the alien ship, though they were doing all the talking. As the junior member of the group, I didn't think any of them would be interested in my theories or speculations. I did find it odd, though, that we had been sitting there for twenty minutes or so and no one had yet mentioned the missing crew members.

Lt. Wu had made that last comment. She had a large cup of coffee on the table in front of her, but she didn't seem interested in drinking any of it. She just held it gently, as though warming her hands, and watched the steam rise.

Lt. Freeman chuckled. "A pirate trap?" he repeated, his deep, resonant voice loaded with humor. "Em, you've got pirates on the brain."

Em? I thought. Short for Emily, perhaps? Lt. O'Malley had introduced them to me by their ranks, not by their first names, and I hadn't gotten around to checking the ship's manifest to learn them.

O'Malley looked over at me, a slight smile on his face. "Her father was a Guardsman, too," he explained. "He was lost years ago, when Lt. Wu was just a child, in an engagement with the pirates. Ever since she joined us she's had a tendency to see pirates in every system."

For just a moment I was tempted to speak up. After Brighthome, pirates were among the few topics I felt qualified to comment on. But I didn't. I knew that anything I said right then would sound self-serving at best. At worst—well, it didn't matter. I'd learned enough on Brighthome to know when to keep my mouth shut. Usually, anyway.

Lt. Wu looked up from her coffee. "And I've been right quite a few times," she said.

"True," Lt. Freeman said, "but you've been wrong a lot, too. And you're wrong this time, Em. Think about it. That ship didn't merely accelerate away from us. It disappeared. Which means either it has some type of jump capability we've never seen, or it has the technology to make it actually disappear. Either way, can you imagine what the pirates would be like if they had those abilities? We'd never get close to them, and we certainly wouldn't have Old Jack himself in custody."

I agreed with Lt. Freeman, and from the look on his face it was clear that O'Malley did, too, but Lt. Wu shook her head. "Not necessarily, John," she said. "For one thing, it's obvious that the pirates didn't build that ship. It was a genuine alien artifact. But that doesn't mean that the pirates might not have discovered it, and learned how to operate it. Without understanding how it works, though, they wouldn't be able to spread the technology to the rest of their ships."

Lt. Freeman—John, I thought—chuckled again. "Em," he said, "listen to yourself. Maybe this and maybe that, except none of it makes any sense. If the pirates had this kind of technology, even if they didn't understand it, don't you think Old Jack would have been using it? If he'd been on that ship, we'd never have taken him at Brighthome."

Lt. Wu started to speak, but John Freeman held up his hand. "Besides, Em, why would the pirates set up a trap here, of all places? We're not near any established travel lanes. No one comes this way. It'd be like setting a bear trap in the middle of a desert. It just doesn't make sense."

Her expression made it clear that she still wasn't convinced, and from what Lt. O'Malley had said about her father I thought I could understand where she was coming from. At a guess, she had probably joined the Space Guard specifically to fight the pirates. With Old Jack captured, people assumed that the pirates would be less of a threat than they had been, which changed everything for her. It made sense that she would cling to her old views for as long as possible.

I smiled, then, inwardly laughing at myself. I'd fallen

into this habit back on Brighthome, building elaborate backgrounds for people on very little information. I suspected that I was wrong far more than I was right, but that hadn't stopped me from doing it. It had made me feel like I knew my fellow students, and had been one of my methods for dealing with the loneliness and the isolation. And now here I was, on board the *Michelangelo*, falling into old habits as easily as I accused Lt. Wu of doing the same thing.

No one at the table noticed my amusement. They were too caught up in their own conversation to pay any attention to me, and for once I was glad of that. I wouldn't have wanted them to think I was laughing at them, but I also wouldn't have wanted to explain what I was thinking.

My thoughts turned sad then and I allowed their conversation to flow over me and past me. For a while I wasn't a part of it. I simply sat back in my chair and watched the three of them interact. This was what I missed, I realized. Watching the three of them, it was easy to replace their faces with Jamie's and Alex's and mine. But those days had gone, perhaps forever, and much of it was my fault.

I smiled again, but this one held no humor in it. Only a tinge of bitterness.

Rising to my feet, I thanked the lieutenants and headed out of the mess hall. Maybe I couldn't rebuild what I had lost, but I had to try.

Maya answered my knock. Her face was guarded when she answered the door, and her expression hardened even further when she saw it was me.

"Tom," she said. Her voice was completely flat and yet it still managed to convey just how displeased she was to see me.

"Hi, Maya," I said, making sure that my own tone was light and pleasant. "Is Alex here?"

Maya shook her head. "She was here a while ago, just long enough to shower and change after her workout, but I haven't seen her since."

"Good," I said.

She blinked at that, one of the few times I'd caught her off guard. "Good?" she repeated.

"Yeah," I said. "Look, Maya, can we talk? It seems you and I got off on the wrong foot somehow, and I'd like to go back and make a fresh start."

I wanted to say more. I wanted to tell her how much Alex meant to me. I wanted to tell her that Alex was my friend, first and foremost, and that everything else that I hoped she would be was based on that friendship. And, most of all, I wanted to tell Maya that I was no threat to her, that my relationship with Alex—whatever it turned out to be—did not have to affect their friendship.

I wanted to say all that, and more, but I never got the chance.

Maya's face hardened further and she shook her head. "I don't know what they taught you in that penal colony," she said. "I understand that Brighthome is built on the concept of second and third chances. But life's not like that. You can't go back, Tom. We are who we are, and there just isn't anything to talk about."

With that, she shut the door in my face. She didn't slam it—the doors on the *Michelangelo* weren't built for slamming—but she shut it with a finality that echoed deep within me.

I stood there, stunned. Was that what this was all about, I wondered? I had thought that Maya didn't like me because she felt threatened by me, but maybe I was wrong. Maybe her feelings were based on nothing more than simple prejudice—I came from Brighthome and therefore I was inherently inferior.

I had expected to run into this when I first decided to join up with the Guard, and I had prepared for that as best I could. But I had been aboard the *Michelangelo* for almost four weeks now, and this was my first taste of it. In that time I had let my guard down. Seeing it now, experiencing it firsthand, I was no longer ready for it, and I felt a sudden, fierce rage flow over me.

Who was she, I thought, to judge me? How could she presume to know who I was or what I had done or what I could become?

This wasn't over, I knew. I had come here hoping to make a friend. Instead, I had found an enemy. So be it.

Spinning on my heel, I headed back to my bunk, fuming all the way.

Chapter Nineteen

I stormed down the corridor toward my room, ready to take on the world—and also ready to have it out with Jamie. It had occurred to me as I made my way back from Alex's quarters that he really wasn't being fair to me. He was mad at me because I had branched out a bit, meeting some new people here on board the *Michelangelo* and establishing the beginnings of some new friendships. And while I could understand how that might bother him, it wasn't really all that different from what he had done back on Brighthome, hooking up with the pirate wannabes there and leaving me to fend for myself.

Of course, I did know other people there myself, and had my own routine established, and here on the *Michelangelo* neither of us had had the time to do that. But still, it just wasn't fair for him to react like he did. And I intended to tell him that.

I didn't get the chance. When I entered our quarters, Jamie was sitting on his bunk, staring at the computer workstation across the room. He seemed relaxed, for the first time in a while, and he turned to look at me as I came in.

"I got it," he said.

I stopped, my anger and resolve utterly deflated. "You what?" I asked.

"I got it," he repeated.

"Good," I said. "Got what?"

He rolled his eyes at that, but I could tell that his exasperation was mostly feigned. It felt good to have the old Jamie back.

"What have I been working on, Tom?" he asked. "I figured out how to enhance the sensor reports."

That got my attention. "The alien ship?" I asked.

He nodded. "I think so. Tell me what you think," he added, indicating the computer monitor.

I headed over to it slowly, unsure what to expect. I was afraid that the screen would be filled with a bunch of undecipherable numbers, or a display of wavy lines or something that I couldn't make sense of. But Jamie had configured the output so that even I could make sense of it. He'd set it up to show the star field in front of the *Michelangelo*. I could even make out the tiny figure of the runabout Alex had been piloting. But I couldn't see the alien ship anywhere.

I studied the screen for a few minutes and then looked back at Jamie. "Nice," I said. "What is it?"

He grinned and rolled off his bunk. Tugging at his jumpsuit to straighten it, he came over to me and started pointing to different controls.

"This is a visual representation of the sensor inputs, starting from when the runabout first left the *Michelangelo* and ending five seconds after the alien ship disappeared. This button will scroll backwards in time; this button moves forward, and this slide here controls the rate. Push it up and the scene moves faster; pull it down and everything goes slower. Right now it's set for real time."

I nodded and reached for the controls. Three times I viewed the final scene at normal speed, but didn't see anything new. The crewmen went out, the remote unit went over, the ship disappeared. Then I slowed it down, moving it to a point a fraction of a second before the ship vanished and scrolling it forward at the slowest possible speed.

I still didn't see anything.

Looking over at Jamie, I shrugged and took my hands off the controls. "There's nothing there," I said.

He grinned again. "That was unenhanced," he said. "Those are the images the bridge crew has been working with, and you're right, there's nothing there." He reached out and hit a sequence of keys. "Now try it."

I reached for the keyboard once more, resetting the rate of display to real time. As the scene played out, I paid careful attention, especially as the moment approached for the ship to disappear.

The moment came, and I thought I saw something, a slight blurring just as the alien vessel vanished.

"What was that?" I asked.

Jamie looked at me. "You've got good eyes, Tom," he said. "I couldn't see it at that speed."

I shrugged again. "Yeah, but I don't know what I'm seeing. You do."

"I think I do," he corrected. He set the scene to the instant right before the ship blinked out and then reset the rate of display to the slowest level. "Watch," he said, and started scrolling forward once more.

I didn't have long to wait. I expected to see a hint of movement, perhaps the beginning of an acceleration in a given direction. I was wrong. Before my eyes, the alien vessel seemed to stretch slightly, and then it simply disappeared.

I blinked and replayed what I had just seen, but I didn't learn anything new. Even at the slowest setting that slight stretching only stayed on the screen for a moment.

I paused it just as the ship was starting its stretch.

"What," I asked, pointing at the image on the display, "is that?"

"That," Jamie said, "is a ship jumping."

I looked at him. "What do you mean?"

All humor was gone from him now. "I don't know," he said, and I could hear a slight note of frustration in his voice. "I've got a piece of something here, Tom, and I can see the barest beginnings of the outline of something new and wonderful, but I don't know what it is or how it works."

He'd lost me with that. He must have been able to tell that from my expression because he gave a helpless little shrug and said, "Let me back up. First of all, what I've done here is to take the sensor logs from both the *Michelangelo* and the runabout and run them through a series of computer enhancements. I took the original logs, enhanced them, and then fed them back through as though the enhanced version was the original. Nothing new—that's standard procedure, after all—except I found a way to tweak the enhancement program a little bit. Not much, but it added a little something to each cycle of enhancement, so that when I was done I had a bit more detail than before."

I nodded to show that I was with him so far.

"Okay," he said. "That's what I *did*. The real question, though, is what I found."

I nodded again. He was exactly right. That's what I wanted to know, and it was what Captain Browne was going to want to know, too.

"If I'm right," he said, "and you've got to understand, Tom, that I'm way out of my element here, but if I'm right, what we're seeing is this ship somehow translating itself to another part of the universe. Instantaneous travel."

"Wow," I said. Then, a moment later, "How?"

He shrugged. "I have no idea."

I looked at him. "I don't believe you."

He held my gaze for a moment, his face unreadable, and then he sighed and looked away. "All right," he said.

"I have an idea, but I'm not ready to talk about it yet, okay?"

I nodded. "Okay, buddy," I said. "So, what now?"

"Now I think we go to the captain. I did a vector analysis on that stretching motion and I learned something else. That stretching is not uniform, Tom. It occurs along a precise axis."

I blinked as I absorbed what he'd said. "A precise axis?" I repeated. "You mean there's a direction to it?"

He nodded.

"So we can tell which direction it went?"

"Sort of," he said. "The problem is that the stretching is constant in both directions along the axis. Which means that we can assume it traveled along a certain line, but I can't yet tell which direction it went on that line or how far along that line it travelled."

I sighed. "Ouch."

"Hey, look, a couple of hours ago we had no idea where that ship went. Now we think we can narrow it down to two possible routes. I'd say that's worth more than an 'ouch.'"

"You're right," I said, clapping him on the shoulder, "and I'm sorry. You've done something really special here, Jamie, and I'm truly impressed. And I agree, my friend. It's time to take this to the captain."

He nodded. "Let's go."

Chapter Twenty

Captain Browne looked at Jamie. "You what?" he asked. Around him, the normally quiet bridge crew had fallen utterly silent. Alex was there, too. She wasn't standing watch, but I wasn't surprised to see her there. I assumed she was simply observing, monitoring the search in the desperate hope that there would be something she could do to help.

"I think I found something that may be of help, sir," Jamie repeated.

He was nervous, I could tell, and the captain's reaction hadn't helped. But I couldn't really blame Captain Browne. He had his best people working on this, and yet it was Jamie, the newest and youngest member of the crew, who had made the breakthrough discovery. I'd have been skeptical, too, in his place.

"Please, sir," Jamie went on, "if I could just show you." He gestured toward one of the bridge monitors.

The captain hesitated and then nodded. "Show me, Apprentice," he said, "and make it good."

Jamie did just that. It only took him a few moments to patch into the program he'd set up.

"It's a recursive routine, sir," he said. "I took the sensor

100

data through several iterations, enhancing the output each time."

Captain Browne nodded. "You know, of course, that we do that, too. It's standard procedure when analyzing any data logs."

"Yes, sir, but I found a way to improve the computer's performance during the enhancement step. Here, sir. Watch."

Jamie didn't bother showing the captain the unenhanced version. He knew as well as I did that everyone on the bridge had viewed that sequence any number of times already. Instead, he froze the display at the very moment where the alien ship started to stretch.

"There, sir," he said. He hit a couple more controls and a vivid red line appeared on the screen, neatly bisecting the alien vessel. "That's the vector, sir. Expansion is uniform in both directions."

Captain Browne tore his eyes from the display long enough to glance at Jamie. "Both directions, eh?" he asked. "So, if this is accurate, we've got a fifty-fifty chance of knowing which way they went."

I was impressed. He'd grasped both the explanation and the implications immediately.

"Yes, sir," Jamie replied. "That's how I see it."

"Lt. Evans," the captain called to the officer stationed at the scanner controls, "look over these program changes. I want to know if they hold up. Ensign McMichaels, I want you to make a study of this display. I want an analysis of that vector. I want to know exactly where that line points, in both directions." His eyes flicked over to me and then settled on Jamie. "Good work, Apprentice," he said. "Excellent work."

"Thank you, sir," Jamie said, but the captain had already turned and gone back toward his post.

"Come on," I said to Jamie. "Let's go get a cup of coffee or something."

He nodded, but that was as far as we got. Before we

could even head toward the two large airlock doors that sealed the bridge off from the rest of the ship, Ensign Lowenstein, the second shift communications officer, held up his hand.

"Incoming signal, sir," he said. "It's a distress call, fading fast." He paused a moment, listening carefully, and then said, "It's gone, sir." He worked his controls, squeezing every bit of information he could out of the brief signal, and then shook his head. "No ship ID, Captain, and no situation report. The transmission was too short. But I do have the direction the signal came from, and I've piped the data over to the Nav console."

"How far away was the source?" Captain Browne asked.

"I'm not sure, sir," Ensign Lowenstein replied. "The signal was too brief to triangulate. But judging from its strength, I'd say it's approximately three days away at best speed."

"Any other ships in the area, Guardsmen, transports, passenger liners, anything?"

Ensign Lowenstein shook his head. "The nearest vessel is three days' farther out, sir."

That was one of the big problems with space travel, and one of the reasons the implications of Jamie's discovery were so exciting. In an emergency situation— and we had to assume that any ship sending out an aborted distress call was facing a genuine emergency— three days was an eternity. There was every possibility that by the time we arrived—if we did, indeed, respond— the situation would be resolved, one way or the other. But with jump technology, the ability to travel instantly from one place to another, response time could be immediate.

The captain had a difficult decision to make, and for the second time since coming aboard I found myself glad that I was only an Apprentice Guardsman. He had to know that we had little chance of helping that ship, and yet our duty to them was clear. We had to make the attempt. What wasn't so clear was our duty to our missing crewmen, and how to choose between the two conflicting responsibilities.

At three days' distance, we could respond, deal with the situation, and return, and assuming that things weren't too complicated there we could be back within a week. That would leave anywhere from four days to a little over a week before the crewmen's air supply ran out, and a week wasn't much for travel time. If that ship did have jump capability, we had no idea what its effective range might be. And, on top of that, Jamie had only been able to narrow the direction down to one of two possible routes. If we headed off in the wrong way . . .

Captain Brown spoke then, cutting off my thoughts—which was just as well; I hadn't liked the direction they were heading anyway.

"Plot your course, Navigator," he said.

"Course plotted and locked in, sir," Lt. Goodnuv replied.

"Ensign Lowenstein, send a return message. Let them know we're on our way and give them your best guess for our ETA."

"Aye, sir."

Captain Browne looked around the bridge. "I need a volunteer," he said. "I don't want to leave this area unattended. If that ship should return, I want someone here to meet it, and, if at all possible, to retrieve our crew members." His gaze came to rest on Alex. "Any takers?" he asked.

"Yes, sir," Alex said immediately. "I volunteer."

The captain nodded. "Accepted," he said. "But not alone. It could be a long wait, and I want two people on your runabout. Pick someone to accompany you."

She glanced over at me and my heart leaped within me. This was it, I thought. This was our chance to repair our friendship, and perhaps even to move forward.

But her expression never softened, and after a moment she looked back at the captain. "I'd like Ensign Davies to accompany me, sir," she said.

I was stunned. I must have made some sort of noise because I felt Jamie's hand on my shoulder, but I couldn't turn to look at him. All I could see was Alex's cold, hard face, and all my hopes and dreams crumbling into ruin.

Captain Browne nodded. "You've got five minutes, Ensign," he said. "We've got a distress call to answer."

Alex returned his nod and left the bridge, not even glancing in my direction. My hands twitched at my sides, as though to reach out toward her, but it was already too late. She was gone.

Chapter Twenty-One

The next couple of days passed quickly, but I was hardly aware of them. I stood my watches, spent time in the simulator, and even explored the Space Guard's database some more, but mostly I thought about Alex. And not just Alex, either, but Alex alone with Ensign Davies. As hard as I tried to block it out, the image of the two of them embracing in the corridor kept coming back to me.

My dream had ended. I could feel it. She had needed someone and she turned to him. I couldn't really blame her, but I did—I blamed her for not giving me a chance; I blamed her for needing him more than me; in short, I blamed her for not being what I needed her to be.

Which wasn't fair, and I knew it, but knowing it didn't help me change my feelings. Instead, I lost myself in my duties, trying to work myself into a state of exhaustion so that I could at least sleep well each night.

It didn't work.

I wasn't the only one busy during that time. Jamie and Lt. Evans were putting in long hours, trying to refine the changes he'd made in the computer analysis routines. The captain had made it clear that we were only going

to have one shot at going after that alien vessel, and it
was up to them to tell him which direction to head.

The rest of the crew was busy as well. There was a
lot of chatter about this distress call, and just about
everyone on board was convinced that it was a pirate
trap.

I agreed with them. I didn't know any more about
the pirates than they did—in fact, I admitted to myself
that, reputation or no reputation, I probably knew less
than the average crewman. But I did know something,
and this distress call had all the earmarks of one of their
less subtle moves.

And through it all, we faced a mounting sense of
urgency. Shortly after we entered hyperspace heading
toward the distress call, someone had set the ship's
computer to display a timer in the corner of each monitor
on board the *Michelangelo*. That timer was counting
down, a constant reminder of how many hours of oxygen
those three crewmen had left. I didn't know if Captain
Browne had authorized that timer or not, but I knew
that he didn't order it removed.

While we were racing to answer a faint and far-off
distress call, that timer was running down. Wherever our
missing crewmen were, they didn't have a lot of time
left, and neither did we. If we were to find them and
save them, we had to do it soon.

The third day started off well enough. I had an early
watch, and after a quick breakfast and most of a cup
of coffee I found myself back on the bridge. The
captain had not let me fly the *Michelangelo* since we
had first encountered the alien ship, and both Jamie
and Lt. Evans were still exempt from bridge duty while
they worked on refining the computer analysis routines,
so I was filling in at the scanner station. But that was
all right with me. I enjoyed handling the helm of the
Michelangelo, and I was looking forward to flying her

again, but not yet. Not until things had settled down. If they ever did.

We were inbound to a small system that barely showed up on our charts. A brown dwarf sun, it had a single gas giant orbiting it about eight AUs out. That was it. No moons around the planet. No asteroid belt. Not even an Oort cloud of comets. This was a system that had lived out its useful life and now held nothing of interest.

Except the distress call, which we still weren't certain about. We had not picked up any new transmissions. Even close in to the system like this, our sensors and our radios were silent.

I had broadened my bands as far as I could, but nothing unexpected was showing up on my screens. Both the brown dwarf and the gas giant stood out like a Guardsman on Brighthome, but I could find no sign of a vessel in distress.

"It's no good, sir," I said after completing my latest sweep. "If there's a ship there, it's a small one and it's not moving rapidly enough to show up on our screens."

The captain nodded. "Which could mean it really was in trouble," he said.

Or that this really is a pirate trap, I thought. I didn't say that out loud, though. Over the past three days, that thought had been voiced by almost every ranking officer and crewman on board the *Michelangelo*. Captain Browne didn't need to hear it again from me.

"All right," he said. "I'm open to opinions. If the distress call is genuine, we'll find the ship, or what's left of it, with a sector-by-sector search. If it wasn't genuine, however, what can we expect?" He looked at me. "Apprentice Guardsman Jenkins, if you were a pirate, where would you hide?"

I'd thought about this a lot in the past three days. But then I'd thought about a lot of things in that time, all in a vain effort to keep my mind off Alex.

"Well, sir," I said, "first, I think we have to expect that

this is a trap. There's nothing in this system, sir, nothing to draw any kind of ship. There are no mining opportunities on that gas giant, and no asteroids to attract prospectors. The view here is unassuming, and unlikely to draw a passenger liner. And this system is not near any known travel lanes, so it's unlikely that a legitimate ship in distress would find itself here. And that means pirates. Given that, sir, I think we also have to assume that they received our message."

Captain Browne nodded. "Agreed," he said.

"Which means they knew approximately when we'd arrive—but, more importantly, it also means they know who and what we are. If it was a lone pirate ship, chances are good that they simply fled the system before we got here. If we're looking for pirates, then, I think we're looking for more than one ship."

The captain nodded again. "Very good," he said. "How many, and where would you look?"

I glanced at my display. "There are only two places to hide that I can see, sir. I'd put one ship in close orbit to the planet, and another one as close to the sun as I could get. Also, since they knew which direction we'd be coming from and our estimated time of arrival, I'd have synchronized the orbits to put them both in position to attack us simultaneously."

His eyes flicked to the Nav console and then back to me. "Anything else?" he asked.

"Yes, sir," I said. "I don't believe that even two ships would be enough—and I don't think the pirates think so, either. I would expect a minimum of three ships, sir, and I would hide the third one either here," I indicated a small area on the screen, "or here. Those positions are both out-system, and either one would put a ship in position to sneak in behind us as we entered the system. That would work even better if they were expecting us to be focussing our sensors in front of us, searching for a disabled ship, rather than watching for a sneak attack from our rear."

"Nicely reasoned, Apprentice," the captain said, "but you overlooked something. Mr. Lovejoy, would you care to explain?"

"Sir," Lt. Lovejoy said from his seat at the Pilot station, "in my opinion, Apprentice Guardsman Jenkins was looking at this situation as an isolated incident, not taking into account the fact that we've learned a lot about their methods, and they've learned a lot about ours. For example, sir, they know that in this kind of a situation, we're likely to begin with search pattern Delta, which would take us on this path through the system." He used his finger to trace an elliptical path around the brown dwarf. "They don't have to attack us when we first enter the system, either. If they've picked their hiding spots with care—and we must assume that they have—they can wait until we've spent hours or days searching, when tedium and exhaustion have dulled our concentration, and then strike."

"I agree, Mr. Lovejoy," the captain said. "So where would you hide, if you were them?"

He indicated his screen again. "I agree with the apprentice that we have to expect at least three ships. If I was in command of their strike force, I would deploy here, here, and here. Each of those positions are outside of the areas we would be expected to search first, and close enough to each other to offer support in case we do the unexpected."

I frowned and looked at my screen once more. I couldn't argue with Lt. Lovejoy's logic, and I certainly couldn't match his experience, but what he had just said bothered me. It sounded like one of those "We know that they know that we know . . ." kind of things. The pirates knew our methods so they were likely to do this; but they also knew that we knew that they knew our methods, so they were likely to do that instead. But they also knew . . .

The chain of who knew what could stretch out forever.

How could the lieutenant —or Captain Browne, for that matter—say where it should end? How could he choose a course of action upon something as vague as that?

I held my tongue, though. I was, admittedly, a novice at all this. But I couldn't help feeling frustrated.

"Lieutenant," the captain said, "take us in, search pattern Delta, but keep your speed up. Apprentice Guardsman Jenkins, maintain a close watch on all screens. In particular, I want you probing those areas Lt. Lovejoy indicated—but I also want you to search the areas you selected as each one comes within reach of the short range sensors."

"Aye, sir." My acknowledgement echoed Lt. Lovejoy's, and we both set to work.

The air on the bridge grew tense. This wasn't what we had hoped for when we left the area of the alien vessel three days earlier. We had all hoped for a quick resolution—either spotting the disabled ship or springing the trap right away—so that we could deal with the situation and get back to the search for our missing crewmen.

But that wasn't what we had found. Our screens were empty, which meant we were going to have to do this the hard way, and a search like this could take days to complete. And the worst part was that we still didn't know what we would find, a ship in genuine distress or a pirate trap.

Turning my attention back to my screens, I did my best to put those thoughts, and thoughts of Alex alone with Ensign Davies, out of my mind. I had a job to do. People were counting on me, and I couldn't afford the luxury of distractions.

Our first discovery came three hours later, and it wasn't what we had expected at all.

My watch had nearly ended when I picked up something faint on my long-range sensors.

"Contact, sir," I said. I read off the bearing information, automatically translating it in my head. The contact, whatever it was, was faint and far-off. It was coming from a spot a third of the way around the sun from our current position, about five times as far out as the gas giant, and slightly below this system's elliptic.

I would have liked to have been able to provide the captain with even more information, like the size and probable classification of the contact. At the very least I would have liked to let him know if it was even a ship, but that was one of the contradictions inherent in life aboard a Space Guard vessel. Protocols demanded that all sensor contacts be reported immediately, without waiting for identification or even confirmation. Guardsman tradition, however, demanded that each report be as complete as possible. Tradition even went further than that. Because Guardsmen were all supposed to be independent problem solvers and troubleshooters, half the time we were expected to offer proposed solutions whenever we reported a problem.

I hadn't gotten to that point yet, and there were days when I thought I never would. In this situation, I didn't hesitate. There were people on that bridge who were much better equipped to deal with this situation than I, and I wanted to get as much information as possible to them as quickly as I could.

"Acknowledged and logged," the captain said. "Mr. Lovejoy, take us there."

"Aye, sir," the pilot said as I fed the course information to both the Navigation and helm consoles.

Our current trajectory through the system was nearly ninety degrees away from the area where the contact was. Under Lt. Lovejoy's guidance, the *Michelangelo* swung around, changing course and heading toward an intercept.

"New heading engaged, sir," the pilot said. "ETA forty-three minutes."

"Acknowledged, Helm," Captain Brown said. "Keep

your sensors sharp, Apprentice." That last bit was directed at me.

"Aye, sir." That would be an easy order to follow, I thought. I'd been doing just that ever since we neared this system. Suspicious of a trap, I'd set up my board to pipe a copy of the sensor feed directly to Jamie and Lt. Evans. They were still working on the computer's analysis routines, and I'd figured they could use some fresh data to work with. Besides, whatever was out there—a ship in distress or a pirate trap—I wanted as much information as our computers could provide.

"Captain," I said as a read-out on my panel came alive. "Spectrographic analysis coming in." I read the data as it scrolled across the tiny screen. When the last of the sparse information had passed, I hit the acknowledgement signal to log in the report and said, "It's definitely a ship, sir. Absorption lines rule out any natural body, but there's no discernible EMF activity. It's either heavily shielded or without power."

So it was a ship. Spectrographic analysis had been able to look at the reflected light coming off the object and by examining which wavelengths had been absorbed they had been able to make a precise assessment of the elements that made up its outer surface. The question now was what kind of ship it was—a ship of the line, either a passenger liner or a freighter or a scout ship, perhaps, or a pirate ship lying in wait.

I would have liked to go to active sensors. Even a single pulse from our forward array would have given us much more information about the object. But I couldn't. Standard rules of engagement in a situation like this required the captain's expressed permission to use active sensors, and I had the feeling that Captain Browne was not yet ready to give that order.

In dealing with the pirates, the Space Guard's strategy was formulated on a single premise: that the pirates' detection equipment wasn't as good as ours. And, so far anyway, that premise had held up. Which was a good thing, because it was just about the only advantage we had against them.

We were assuming that any pirates in the area knew we were there. We had sent a signal announcing our ETA, and we were moving fast enough that even the oldest sensor arrays would have picked up our arrival in-system. But we were assuming that they didn't know precisely where we were, or what our heading was—which was why I was certain the captain would not authorize the use of actives. One pulse would tell us a lot about that object out there, and might turn up a pirate ship or two lurking nearby, but it would also pinpoint our position and provide targeting data to any enemy ships in the area.

All of which might be moot, I knew. If there were any pirates around, they knew we'd be heading toward that silent vessel. The closer we came to it, the more precisely they'd be able to locate us.

And that was the part that really complicated this situation: the fact that we'd received a distress signal and that there was a ship drifting dark and silent in this system. If all we had to worry about was pirates, the captain's strategy would have been far different, I knew. He'd have probably slowed considerably while we were still out-system. He also might have sent in one or more shuttles to reconnoiter. At the very least, he would have launched several sensor buoys.

But that ship out there changed all that. Our first priority now was rescue, which meant we had to make best time to that ship. We didn't have the luxury of playing it safe. We just had to rush in with our eyes open and our guard up.

When we were thirty minutes out, Captain Browne gave the command to man battle stations. There was a brief flurry of activity as all off-shift personnel scrambled to get into their space suits, though none of them would actually seal up their helmets unless an actual battle broke out. Those of us on-shift set up a brief, five-minute rotation, allowing each of us to get into our own suits while keeping all the stations manned.

The feel of my helmet clipped to the back of my locking collar was unfamiliar to me, and more than a little distracting. I hadn't worn my suit before, except to try it on for size after it was tailored, and I found that putting it on didn't fill me with the same sense of excitement and adventure that I'd once thought it would. Instead, what I felt mostly was fear.

Explosive decompressions were rare, even in battle. Hulls were breached frequently, but every ship was designed to seal itself in an emergency, blocking off damaged areas and keeping as much air in as possible. The thought that the bridge itself, or any of the interior decks of the *Michelangelo*, could be vented into space . . . well, that thought didn't exactly fill me with confidence.

My gloved fingers were slightly stiff as I worked my controls, but that was mostly because my suit hadn't been broken in yet. Given time, and a little practice, I'd be as smooth and fluid in my motions as my shipmates.

"Sir," I said, scanning my board. "More data coming in. Preliminary readings of its size, mass, and configuration indicate that it's a small freighter or possibly a no-frills passenger liner. There are burn marks near the rear drive section, sir, a clear sign that this ship was in a battle, and lost." I kept scanning the information as it rolled across my screen, passing it on to the captain as quickly as it came in. "There are no weapons mounted on the hull, sir, and no signs that any were removed. If there was a battle, Captain, it was pretty one-sided. She was a sitting duck."

Lt. Evans, seated at my left, glanced over at my board, as if to confirm my readings, but he didn't say anything.

"We're still not picking up any energy readings," I said,

"and there's no sign of a ship's registry, no beacon, nothing to indicate what this ship is or where it's from."

"Could be a pirate ship," Lt. Evans said. "Maybe they're baiting this trap themselves."

"Perhaps," the captain said. "Mr. Jenkins, keep close watch on that ship. I want to know the instant she shows any sign of life."

"Aye, sir," I said.

And they were right, pirate ships did tend to go unmarked, though many times they simply didn't bother to remove the original registry from any ship they hijacked. But something was bothering me, something I'd known once, or had heard somewhere, that was nagging at the back of my thoughts. Something about unmarked ships . . .

I couldn't pin it down, though, and after a few moments things got busy enough that I couldn't pursue it.

At twenty minutes out, the captain gave the order to launch two runabouts. Lieutenants Wu and Freeman were at the helms, and each ship carried a complement of six Guardsmen to man the onboard weapon systems. The two shuttles accelerated away from us, spreading out to provide as much cover for us as they could.

"Mr. Jenkins, I want sensor feeds shunted both ways between those shuttles. I want to see everything they see, and I want them to have full access to all our data."

"Aye, sir." My fingers were still a bit stiff, but it only took me a moment to set up the bridges he'd called for. I also set it up so that the incoming signals were routed down to Jamie as well. "Feeds in place, sir," I said. "Data coming in." I scanned the information quickly and then added, "No new contacts, sir."

"Acknowledged."

At ten minutes out, Captain Browne looked at Lt. Evans. "All stop, Helm," he said.

That order took a little while to carry out. We'd been

decelerating slowly as we neared our target, but we still had a fair bit of momentum that Lt. Evans had to kill.

A few moments later, Lt. Evans said, "Helm answers all stop, sir. All motion is zero relative to our target."

"Very good, Helm," the captain said. He looked around the bridge, and his gaze settled on me. "Apprentice Guardsman Jenkins," he said. "Report to the hangar bay. I need you to take a boarding party over to that ship. Your instructions, Mr. Jenkins, are to stay with your shuttle and to exercise extreme caution."

"Aye, sir," I said. Rising to my feet, I snapped a quick, heartfelt salute, and then headed off the bridge. As I left, I was surprised to see the captain himself moving over to take up my station.

"Good luck, Mr. Jenkins."

"Thank you, sir," I said as the massive doors slid shut behind me.

Inside my suit, my palms were sweating with nervousness and anticipation. I knew that the captain had selected me for this mission out of necessity—there weren't any other qualified pilots on board—but that didn't matter. This was my chance to show him what I could do, and I wasn't about to let him down.

Resolve hardening within me, I hurried on to the hangar bay.

Chapter Twenty-Two

Captain Browne had ordered the entire hangar bay depressurized so that the shuttles could depart faster. I sealed up my suit before cycling through the airlock.

I had expected to find the boarding party waiting for me on the other side, but only the team leader was there. Through his visor, I could see that he had dark hair cut short, brown eyes, and a thin mustache. He wore the three stars of a lieutenant emblazoned on his helmet, the name Ramirez stenciled on the left breast of his suit, and an air of arrogance that I immediately disliked. Not that it mattered all that much whether I liked Lt. Ramirez or not. He was the senior officer in charge of this mission, but he had little authority over me. I was the pilot. The shuttle was my responsibility, and all decisions concerning the flight were left to my sole discretion.

Ramirez barely glanced at me, his eyes tracking over my name and my lack of any rank insignia, and then he turned his back on me. "We're in here, Apprentice," he said, gesturing toward one of the two remaining shuttles parked in this hangar. "Let's get going."

I stiffened slightly. That was a breach of protocol, and

I was sure that the lieutenant knew it. The question was, did he have something out for me personally, or was this simply his way of acknowledging that we were on an important mission and that time was of the essence? I would have liked to have assumed the latter, but I didn't dare. I'd been through this too many times on Bright-home, and I had the feeling I was about to go through it again.

The thing was that, as the pilot, it was my job to select which ship we would take, not his. I would have been within my rights to countermand him. If I had wanted to make an issue of it, I could have selected the other ship, and forced his crewmen to debark and reboard the other shuttle, but I didn't. It wasn't worth it. Until I had flown all the different shuttles, and flown them enough to learn their individual traits, they were all the same to me, and one was as good as another.

Still, I filed this incident away in the back of my mind. Lieutenant Ramirez had shown his true colors to me, and I wasn't about to forget. That old, familiar churning in my belly wouldn't let me.

I followed the lieutenant onto the shuttle, sealing the door behind me. Normally I would have started the pressurization cycle, too, but not this time. With the potential for conflict on this mission, standard procedure was to keep the oxygen in the tanks. That would help minimize damage in the event of a hit.

Glancing around, I saw that counting Ramirez there were a total of twelve Guardsmen in the boarding party itself. A couple of them nodded at me as I made my way toward the controls, but there simply wasn't time for any introductions.

"Skip the pre-flights," the lieutenant said as he strapped himself in to the navigator's seat to the right of my station. "We're in a hurry."

That was too much. I slid into my own seat and then turned to look at him. "Negative, sir," I said.

Under other circumstances, I would have replied on a private channel, but not this time. He had used the frequency assigned to our team, meaning that the eleven Guardsmen strapped in behind us had heard every word he'd spoken to me since I entered the hangar bay. I used the same frequency to reply.

His dark eyes flashed with sudden anger and locked on mine. "What did you say, Apprentice?" he asked, still on the public frequency. That stripped away the last of my doubts about his motives. If he'd truly been concerned about the mission, rather than simply trying to put me in my place, he would have either accepted my answer or switched to a private channel.

"I said negative to skipping the pre-flights, sir. It is neither safe nor necessary in this situation. In my opinion, sir."

His mouth curled in a half smile, half sneer. "Your opinion?" he repeated. "You're an Apprentice Guardsman. You're not entitled to an opinion. Now carry out your orders, Apprentice."

"No, sir," I said. "On this mission, I am the pilot, and we will follow standard procedures unless, in my opinion, circumstances warrant otherwise." Up to now, I thought I had done a pretty good job of keeping my own anger in check, but I couldn't resist adding one more shot. "For instance, sir," I said, "as you know, protocol is for the team leader to be seated with his crewmen, not at the Navigator station. But I'm willing to make an exception, Lieutenant, as long as you do not interfere with my flying."

He glared at me, and for a moment I thought he was going to switch to a private channel at last, but he didn't. He merely nodded, his eyes still locked on mine. "All right, Apprentice," he said. "Conduct your pre-flights, but make it fast. We've got a mission to accomplish."

"Aye, sir," I said. Breaking eye contact, I turned my attention to my board and quickly ran through the pre-flight checks. I tried to put our little exchange out of my mind, but I couldn't. I knew that I would replay these past few minutes in my mind over and over, looking for other ways I could have handled it, second-guessing myself, and finding fault with every word I'd said. I'd done the right thing, I was sure of that, but I was equally sure that I had just made my first real enemy on board.

When my pre-flight checks were completed, I gave the command to open the hangar doors and gently powered up. It was a moment I should have relished— my first time solo at the controls of a runabout since leaving Brighthome—but the moment had been spoiled.

With a conscious effort, I brought my attention back to the mission at hand and took the little ship out into space.

Chapter Twenty-Three

For the first few minutes of the flight, my attention was completely taken up by my duties. This shuttle was newer and more complete than the runabout I had claimed as my own back on Brighthome, and while I had spent some time in the simulator recently, no simulator ever built was exactly the same as the real thing.

Once I was satisfied with the way the ship handled, I initiated the direct sensor feed back to the *Michelangelo* and to the two shuttles flying support. Then, and only then, was I free to turn my attention to the beauties of space.

It was breathtaking. The brown dwarf was behind us, somewhere over my right shoulder, and so I had an unrestricted view of the stars themselves, and what a view it was. The stars were sharp and brilliant, shining red and blue and white wherever I looked, and there was a sensation of depth to the view, a feeling of being physically out there among the stars, that never came through a view port.

The vessel we were approaching was still too far away to be visible. That was all right, though. I'd taken its position directly from the *Michelangelo*'s onboard systems, and had the shuttle flying straight toward the ship.

Lt. Ramirez was the first to spot our target.

"There she is," he said, pointing toward the main view screen.

I glanced up, still keeping most of my attention on my board. The ship was barely visible at the center of the screen. A faint spot of reflected light, it was just large enough to be noticeable among the sea stars.

"What's our ETA, Apprentice?" he asked.

I automatically checked our speed and position before answering. "A little over three minutes," I said.

Ramirez frowned, but didn't say anything. Reaching out, he manipulated the controls in front of him, magnifying the scene on the view screen and zooming in on the ship.

I assumed he was looking for a place to dock—which was fine with me. I was still busy flying the ship and keeping an eye out for signs of a trap. I could use a little help.

As the ship grew larger on the screen, I glanced up for a moment and suddenly froze, my hands motionless on my controls.

The lieutenant noticed immediately. "What is it, Apprentice?" he asked. "What's wrong?"

But I couldn't answer. Not right away, anyway.

"Dammit, Jenkins," he said, "what is it? What do you see? Pirates?"

I shook my head, the momentary paralysis slipping away. "I know that ship," I said.

And it was true. It was impossible, but it was true. I had memories that only stretched back four years, to the day a Guardsman ship found me drifting in an unmarked survival pod. Since that time, I'd been on a handful of ships—and none of them were the one drifting before us now. And yet I recognized that ship. Not with my head—I couldn't name it, or say where it was from, or where it was heading—but somewhere, deep down inside of me, there had been a moment of sudden recognition when I saw it there on the screen.

Ramirez swivelled his head to look at me. "What do you mean?" he asked.

"I don't know," I said honestly. I didn't think I could put all my vague feelings into words, and I certainly didn't want to try. Not just yet, and not with him. "Just a feeling, sir. Déjà vu, I guess."

He glared at me. "I'm not interested in your feelings, Apprentice," he said. "Just do your job and get us to that ship."

"Aye, sir," I said.

"There," he added, pointing at the image on the screen. "We'll board there." He'd selected the aft section of the ship. There was a lot of damage back there, but the service port he was pointing at seemed intact.

I nodded. It was as good a choice as any, though I'd half expected him to split his team, one group boarding in the rear and the rest entering the ship near the bow. But that was why he was leading this mission. There were probably some sound tactical reasons that I knew nothing about for not allowing his forces to be split.

"A Group," he said, still on the team frequency, "prepare to board. Johnson, Hanks, look sharp. This is when we'll be the most vulnerable to attack." Ramirez turned back to me. "I'll board with A Group," he said. "After we're clear, take the ship to this point," he indicated a spot near the nose of the ship. "B Group will board here. When they're safely on board, take up station here," he moved his finger to a spot midway down the ship's hull, "and wait for a recall signal from either group."

So he would be splitting his group after all. I hid my grin and acknowledged his orders. "Aye, sir," I said. "A Group here, B Group here, maintain station here. Understood, sir."

"We're counting on you, Apprentice," he said. "Don't let us down."

I turned and looked at him, but I didn't reply. There was nothing to say.

Moments later we reached the first boarding point. With the shuttle depressurized, there was no reason to extend the airlock tunnel, so A Group merely tethered themselves to the hull and crossed over a few meters of empty space to the other ship. I kept a close eye on my board, while several other crewmen watched other read-outs. The lieutenant was right: this was when we were most vulnerable, now and when we offloaded B Group, and we had to keep a sharp lookout for attack.

The process went smoothly, with no sign of pirates, and in less than a minute the half dozen members of A Group had vanished within the depths of the drifting vessel.

Under other circumstances we would have sent a remote unit in first, but that simply wasn't an option this time. We were pretty sure that the distress call was a fake and that this was all an elaborate trap, but without any solid evidence of that we had to act on the possibility that it was genuine. And that meant sending a boarding party in immediately. If there were any passengers or crew on that ship, and if any of them were still alive, they'd need rescuing and medical attention that a remote unit simply couldn't provide.

"We're in," Lt. Ramirez's voice came over the radio in my helmet. "Proceed."

"Acknowledged, sir," I said. "Good luck."

Ramirez didn't answer. I hadn't expected him to, but I couldn't help feeling a bit angry as I took the shuttle to the next boarding point.

B Group was every bit as fast as A Group. I'd wondered if Ramirez would leave any Guardsmen on board the shuttle to man the weapons, but he didn't. The remaining six crewmen all crossed over to the ship while

I did my best to watch for any sign of trouble. One of them, Johnson, perhaps, radioed when they were safely aboard. I acknowledged, and slowly backed the shuttle away.

Within two minutes I was on station. I sent a signal to the boarding party informing them, and then turned my attention to my scanners. We were expecting trouble, and that had me worried. The pirates—assuming they really were around—had already passed up their best shot at us, which meant that either this wasn't a trap after all, or they had something much sneakier and much more deadly in mind.

In situations like this, we always had to assume the worst. It was now up to me and the scanner operators back aboard the *Michelangelo* to make sure that whatever the pirates had planned didn't come as a surprise.

I scanned my boards, alternating between passive sensor sweeps and visual searches of nearby space, but my eyes kept coming back to the image of that ship. What was it? Where was it from? And, most of all, why did it seem so familiar to me?

There were no answers to be found out there in the silence of space, but the questions wouldn't leave me as I settled in to wait for the recall signal.

Chapter Twenty-Four

It was going to be a long wait, I knew. There wasn't much for me to do except watch my board and monitor the chatter between A Group and B Group, and that passed quickly from exciting to boring. I couldn't recognize any voice other than Lt. Ramirez's, and his wasn't all that interesting.

"Maintain formation, rolling pattern."

"Forward section reached. No sign of casualties."

"Second section reached. No sign of casualties."

I could picture the two groups moving slowly toward each other. With no power available to maintain the artificial gravity well, the Guardsmen would all have activated the magnetic locks on their boots. They'd be moving forward slowly, making sure each step locked onto the floor before breaking the grip with their other foot.

In the airless world of the derelict ship, each step would be soundless, except for the tiny vibrations travelling up through their own bodies to register as tiny seismic shocks within their inner ears.

"Blast doors have been forced here, sir. Looks like they had time to organize some sort of resistance at least, though I can't tell how effective it was."

The ship they had boarded was an ugly thing. Over a hundred meters long, it was broken into three separate sections, all cylindrical in shape and roughly the same size. Not a fast configuration—its acceleration was limited by the amount of stress the two connecting tunnels could take—but it was standard for cargo ships. This design allowed separate storage for volatile materials and perishable goods, and kept everything separated from the drive and crew section.

Somehow, though, I didn't think this was a cargo ship. And that was what was driving me nuts: if it wasn't a cargo ship, what was it? And how did I know?

If there was one advantage to this, it was that it had managed to take my mind off Alex and what might be happening on board her shuttle between herself and Ensign Davies. And that was something that hadn't happened in the past three days.

Still, I would have liked to understand what was going on back there in the farthest corners of my brain. That ship—or one very much like it—meant something to me. I just had no idea what.

My boards still showed clear, and the chatter between the groups had fallen into a routine that I could listen to with only half an ear. With little else to occupy my attention, my thoughts began to drift.

I needed something to do, I realized, something to help keep my concentration focussed, and sitting idly, watching my boards, just wasn't enough, so I decided to give in to an impulse. Setting my board to signal me at the faintest of sensor contacts, and keeping my suit radio tuned to the boarding party's frequency, I used my shuttle's comm link to establish a connection with the databases on board the *Michelangelo*. Splitting my screen so that I could still monitor my scanners, I started scrolling through commentary on ship designs. If that derelict out there wasn't a cargo ship, what was it?

It didn't take me long to find out. There was a brief

passage that listed alternative uses for many of the more
generic ship types, and though I didn't find this particular
configuration anywhere, I did see something that caught
my eye. Listed right after "smuggling" and right before
"piracy" was the word "colonization."

That's it, I thought. *That's a colony ship.* I still had
no idea why I was so sure, but I was, with a certainty
that went beyond mere belief. I *knew* what that ship was.

Without consciously deciding to, I closed my eyes and
turned my attention inward, probing for the source of
that knowledge. I didn't really expect to find anything.
I'd been searching the trackless, featureless wasteland
that was my past for four years now and had never
turned up anything that resembled a real memory. But
something within me forced me to try once again.

*Dark hair, and a loving smile. I saw her face as she
bent over me to kiss me good night. Her lips moved,
forming words that would not take shape in my mind,
and I felt her gentle fingers brush back my hair. In that
moment I knew who she was, who I was, and I recalled
what it felt like to be safe and secure and loved.* Her
image faded, though, slipping through my mental grasp,
and with it went all the knowledge, all the memories it
had brought, leaving only emptiness and sorrow.

A wave of grief washed over me, a sense of pain and
loss that brought sudden sharp tears to my eyes. I waited,
trying to keep my thoughts silent, willing more images
to come, more memories to return, but they didn't.
Casting back into the depths of my mind, I sought
another glimpse of that almost familiar face, but all that
I found were echoes of my pain.

For a long moment I simply sat there, feeling my
heartbeat slow to normal and letting the pieces of my
life fall back into the easy, comfortable patterns they had
formed over the past four years. That face I'd seen had
to have been my mother. I didn't know that, not with
the same non-rational certainty that I knew that ship out

there was a colony vessel, but no other explanation made sense. She was my mother, but I couldn't remember her at all.

Opening my eyes, I glanced down at my board. Nothing had changed, except that my hands were clenched tightly and hovering near the controls.

I didn't have to think hard to interpret that. I knew what I wanted to do. I wanted to hit the jets and redock with that ship. I wanted to leave my shuttle and go exploring, looking for clues to my past. But I couldn't. I had a job to do. My crewmates were counting on me, and Lt. Ramirez would never give me permission to board that vessel.

Closing my eyes again, I focussed on the radio chatter, listening to the reports coming from *A* and *B* Groups as they explored the ship.

"Burn marks all along the corridor here, sir." I couldn't put names to the voices, but that sounded like the point man for *B* Group. "They look like blaster shots. I'd say she was definitely boarded."

Darkness. A sense of confinement and fear. Noises in the background, shouts and alarms and some sort of explosion that might have been a hull breach. Then nothing.

The memory—if that's what it was—slipped away once more, leaving me grasping at smoke. My eyes were stinging, and with my helmet on I couldn't rub them, or even wipe the tears away, but that didn't bother me so much. What bothered me was being this close and not being able to board that ship.

I had to get on board. Somehow, some way, I had to walk those corridors myself. I just had to. But I couldn't.

"There's nothing here, sir." That was the B Group leader again. "The entire drive section has been gutted, and the cargo bay is empty."

"We're in the conn," Lt. Ramirez replied. "Same story here. Whoever boarded her stripped her down pretty good. Everything worth salvaging—every computer, every console, everything of any value at all—has been removed. There's nothing but bulkheads and burn marks left."

"Burn marks? So it looks like a running battle, then, sir?"

"Affirmative. The crew of this ship put up a good fight. But they lost."

My hands were clenched at the sides of my board as visions of the scene bombarded me. This was imagination, not true memory, but it was all too real: a band of space-suited pirates pouring through the breach in the hull, colonists and crew members falling back before them, blaster fire cutting through the chaos.

Was this what had happened to me? Did I disappear from this very ship more than four years ago, or was it a different ship—one very much like this, perhaps, but in a different system, a different quadrant? Or, worse, was this all a false memory, manufactured by my sub-conscious in a desperate attempt to find something to believe in, something to hold on to?

I didn't know. I couldn't know. But I had to know.

"What about survival pods?" I asked, my voice shaky with the strain.

There was a pause, and then Lt. Ramirez answered me, an edge to his voice. "Who is that?" he asked. "Who's speaking on this frequency?"

"It's Jenkins," I said. "Apprentice Guardsman Tom Jenkins. What about survival pods, Lieutenant? Are there any signs that they might have launched their pods?"

Again Ramirez hesitated, and for that brief moment I thought he was going to ignore my question. But he didn't. "Vasquez, Hanks," he said. "Check it out."

It took a couple of minutes for Vasquez and Hanks to locate the pod bays. Those were two of the longest minutes of my life.

"I've found them, sir," one of them, a female, said.

"Four bays, looks like one pod per bay, but they're all gone sir."

"Any launch marks?" I asked. An emergency launch would leave scorch marks on the inside of the bay. Also, the exterior door hinges would show the signs of an emergency blow. If the pods had simply been scavenged, however, there would be no scorch marks and the hinges would be intact.

"Jenkins," Ramirez said, "shut up. Let us do our job." He hesitated, giving me a chance to speak, but I didn't. He was right. "Vasquez, Hanks," he said after a moment, "any launch marks?"

They didn't need long to examine each of the bays, but to me, waiting anxiously for their report, it seemed forever before I heard her say, "Aye, sir. It's hard to tell with all the other damage this ship has taken, but at a guess I'd say that all four pods were launched."

"Then there might have been survivors," I said.

This time Lt. Ramirez didn't hesitate. "Jenkins," he said, "private channel. Now." I switched over, but he didn't give me a chance to speak. "Listen, Apprentice," he said, his voice stern and harsh, "I'm not going to tell you again. We've got a mission to accomplish here, and you're interfering with that mission. As of now, you are on report. One more outburst from you and I'll have your flames revoked."

"But, sir—"

"No," he said. "I know what you're going to say, and you're wrong. We don't know that there were any survivors. The crew of this ship may have simply launched all four pods as a decoy, an attempt to draw their attackers away from their ship. Besides, it's a safe bet that their attackers would have chased down any escape pods."

"So you don't think we should search for any survivors?" I asked.

"No, I don't," he said, "but that's not my decision to

make. And it's not yours, either, Apprentice. All of this information will be in my report, and it will be the captain who decides how to respond."

"Yes, sir," I said. But he was wrong. The more I saw of that ship, the more reports I heard from the boarding party, the more certain I became that there had been at least one survivor from that ship: me.

"Now no more chatter," he said. "And stay off our frequency."

"Yes, sir," I said again. He didn't reply, and I suspected he had switched away from the private channel before I had even replied. I switched over as well, and then sat back in my seat, anger and frustration burning within me.

It just wasn't fair. He was wrong. I knew he was wrong. But there was no way that I could prove it. And there was no way that I could make him listen to me.

I was thinking those thoughts, feeling sorry for myself and mad at him, when another call came in. This one wasn't from Ramirez, though. It was from Jamie.

"Hey, Tom," he said. "You busy?"

I glanced down at my board and then back at the derelict ship drifting dead ahead of me. "I can spare you a few minutes," I said, trying for a little bit of humor. "What's up?"

"I'm not sure," he said. "I'd like to pipe a few images over to you and see what you think."

"Give me a moment." I cleared one of my displays and set it up to receive a visual signal from him. "All right," I said. "Go ahead."

The screen lit up with a view similar to the one I'd been looking at—a field of stars shining brightly against a background of black velvet, only there was no colony ship in this image.

"It's coming through fine," I said. "What am I looking at?"

"The lieutenant and I were working on refining the

computer enhancements I'd made and we decided to run one of the old astrophotography routines—you know, take two separate images of the same region of space, several minutes apart, and then overlay them to see if anything has moved. Well, we did that, and this is what we found. The area you're looking at is directly behind the *Michelangelo*."

He set the signal he was sending me to alternate quickly between two separate images. At least, that's what I assumed he was doing, but it took me a moment to see what he was trying to show me.

"There," I said, pointing to two faint stars near the right edge of the screen. He couldn't see me point, but I did it anyway, automatically. "Those two stars are blinking. They're there in one image, and then gone in the next. Is that what you're talking about?"

"You got it, Tom," he said. "What do you think it means?"

I didn't have to think. I'd done enough reading back on Brighthome to be familiar with this technique. Old time astronomers back on Earth had used it to find asteroids and comets and planets within the solar system. A star that moved was probably a planet. Stars that disappeared in one image and reappeared in another were occluded by something—like a comet or an asteroid. But we'd already searched out this system pretty thoroughly. There *were* no comets or asteroids. Which meant that something else was occluding those stars, and I could only think of one thing that it could be.

"Has Lt. Evans seen these?" I asked.

"No," Jamie said. "He's out getting some fresh coffee. He should be back any minute."

"Don't wait for him," I said. "Call the captain, Jamie. Now."

"Why?" he asked. "What is it?"

"It's a ship, Jamie. It has to be. And I'll lay you odds that it's coming our way."

Chapter Twenty-Five

Pirates, I thought. No other explanation made sense. And I was especially bothered by the fact that our sensors hadn't detected the ship.

There had been rumors back on Brighthome, reports that the pirates had developed—or, more likely, stolen—some sort of cloaking technology, but I had discounted them. True cloaking technology was supposedly impossible. Besides, there were always rumors on Brighthome about how great the pirates were, and how badly they'd beaten the Guard in this encounter or that one. Three quarters of the student population on Brighthome wanted nothing more than to be taken in by the pirates someday, and there was a constant supply of new stories and rumors.

But maybe this one was true—or at least based on a kernel of truth. After all, if the ship possessed a true cloaking device, it wouldn't have occluded any stars. It would simply have passed the light around it and Jamie would never have picked up it. Clearly, then, this ship wasn't cloaked in the truest sense, but equally clearly it had something, some sort of stealth technology, that rendered it invisible to our sensors, and I didn't like that at all.

We'd hoped that the capture of Old Jack himself would put an end to the pirates, but maybe we were wrong. If they did have effective stealth capabilities, then perhaps the war wasn't as close to being over as we'd thought. On the other hand, though, this didn't mean that we had lost, either. Stealth technology would give them a definite advantage in certain situations: it would help them to spy on us; it would help them attack and board freighters, colony ships, and passenger liners; and it would help them lay more effective traps against us— like the one we had just walked into. They had known exactly where we'd be, and thanks to our radio message they'd had a pretty good idea when we'd get there. That allowed their small ships to sneak in slowly enough that they wouldn't show up on the hyperwave grid.

But there were also a lot of situations where the stealth technology wouldn't help them at all. Their ships would show up on our mass detectors if they moved too fast, which meant that their stealth technology was essentially useless in the heat of battle. Also, now that we knew about it, we could employ visual sensing, like the astrophotography routine Jamie had used, to keep them from catching us off-guard again.

Assuming, of course, that we survived this encounter. They were close enough already to jam any message we tried to send to Central, so if we were going to pass the word about their new capabilities, we were going to have to escape their trap.

Jamie had clicked off while I thought about all that. I'd assumed that he'd gone to a different channel to alert the captain. I switched over to the bridge communication frequency and listened in.

" . . . are still showing no significant contacts." That was the captain's voice. "Lt. Evans, can you confirm?"

"Aye, sir." The lieutenant had obviously returned with his coffee. "We'll pipe the images to your display, but I can definitely confirm the apprentice's observations.

Something is blocking out some of the stars. Computer analysis of its motion indicates it's close and heading our way. ETA is thirty minutes."

"Keep on it, Lieutenant," the captain said. "I want as much information as you can provide, and I want it now. But stay with passives only for the time being. They can't know we've discovered them, and I want to keep it that way for as long as possible."

"Aye, sir."

"Apprentice," he said to Jamie, "keep using that astrophotography program to search all around us. If that is a pirate vessel, it won't be alone. I want to know who else is out there and exactly where they are."

He didn't wait for Jamie to acknowledge. An indicator in my helmet indicated that he had switched over to the boarding party frequency. I followed him in time to hear him ask, "Lt. Ramirez, what's your status?"

"*A* and *B* Groups forming up, sir. We've swept the two outermost sections of the ship and are heading toward a rendezvous in the center. Twenty minutes should do it, sir."

"Twenty minutes is too long," the captain said. "You've got ten. I want your people off that ship and back aboard the *Michelangelo* before the fireworks start."

"Aye, sir," Lt. Ramirez said.

"Apprentice Jenkins, maintain your present position until you receive the recall signal," the captain said, "but keep your jets hot. When you make your pickup run, I want you to do it fast and clean."

"Aye, sir," I said. My voice came out calm and confident, which surprised me because that wasn't how I felt at all. Ever since coming aboard the *Michelangelo*, I'd expected that I would eventually take part in a battle with the pirates, but I'd never dreamed it would come so soon, and I certainly hadn't imagined that my role would be quite so large. I figured I'd probably be in my wardroom, following the action on my computer display, or perhaps I'd be in the Observer station on the bridge. Instead, I was at the helm of a shuttle, with a dozen crew members depending on me to get them back to the ship safely.

Thinking about that, and realizing just how important my job had become, I replotted the various courses I had laid in, taking me to the two different pickup points and then back to the *Michelangelo*. I wanted to make sure that I had the most efficient burns calculated, minimizing the travel time as much as possible. I also plotted some alternates, in case Lt. Ramirez ordered a change in the pickup sequence. I was assuming that the boarding party would all be together and would be picked up at one point or the other, but I wanted to be ready for whatever the lieutenant ordered.

Something was bothering me, though. I checked my board carefully, looking for any signs of problems, and found nothing. But that didn't ease that nagging feeling that I had overlooked something.

I frowned, trying to pin it down. Something Jamie had said? I'd already considered the ramifications of stealth ships. There was nothing there to worry me. Not yet, anyway. And both Jamie and Lt. Evans were working hard to spot any other pirate ships closing in on us. With that astrophotography program and Jamie's computer enhancements, I was confident that we'd have a report soon.

So it wasn't that. What then? Something someone else had said?

I set my board to replay snatches of conversation I'd picked up from various members of the boarding party. Maybe there was something about the survival pod, something that Vasquez had said that hadn't registered at the time, or maybe it was someone else. I was careful to make sure that the conversations played in the background, though. I wanted to be able to hear the recall signal when it came.

"Burn marks all along the corridor here, sir."

"There's nothing here, sir."

"I'd say she was definitely boarded."

Lt. Evans' voice broke in to my playback. "Two more ships spotted, sir, bearing oh-four-five and two-seven-oh, both in the ecliptic."

Automatically, I noted the ships' positions on my display. With the one coming in from behind the *Michelangelo*, that put the three ships at the points of a not-quite-equilateral triangle, and that surprised me. I would have expected two of the ships to come in with the brown dwarf and the gas giant at their backs, masking what little ripples they might make on our detectors. But they were nowhere near those bearings, which meant either they were very confident in their stealth capabilities or there was something else I was overlooking.

On a whim, I called up the positions of the other two shuttles, the ones flown by Lts. Wu and Freeman. Glancing at the display, I could see that the pirates had anticipated our defensive formation. Two of their ships were exactly splitting the distance between our pickets. But that third one, that seemed out of place. By rights, it should be coming in close to the derelict colony ship. That route would give it the clearest shot at the *Michelangelo*, and keep it as far away from the supporting runabouts as possible.

That third ship, however, the one bearing 045, was giving the derelict as wide a berth as possible. Either they knew I was here and were playing it safe, or . . .

At that moment, Lt. Ramirez's recorded voice rang out.

"We're in the conn. There's . . ."

That's it, I thought. That's what I'd been missing.

I set my radio to include both the boarding party frequency and the bridge channel. "Lt. Ramirez," I said, "you have to abort the mission."

There was a brief pause, and then the lieutenant said, "Who is this? Jenkins?"

"Yes, sir." I knew his helmet indicator was showing him which channels were open, and he'd have to at least hear me out.

"Look, Apprentice—" he started, but I cut him off.

"No, sir. There's no time. You have to abort the mission. You're walking into a trap."

"What do you mean, Apprentice?" That was the captain speaking.

"Lieutenant," I said, "didn't you say that you made it to the conn and found nothing? That there was 'nothing but bulkheads and burn marks left'?"

"Yes." He stretched that word out slightly, and I knew he didn't see where I was going yet. Maybe that should have made me feel better, but I was still kicking myself for not seeing the obvious sooner.

"But that's not possible," I said. "Not unless it's a trap. We came here because of a distress signal that we assumed came from that very ship. But you were at the conn and there was no power available, and no comm unit to send a signal. It *has* to be a trap. My guess, sir, is that there's a bomb planted on board, and the pirates will detonate it right before they launch their attack on the *Michelangelo*. You have to abort the mission, sir, and you have to do it now."

"Can we jam their signal?" the lieutenant asked.

"Sure," I said, "if they use a standard radio transmitter and receiver. But not if they use a tighter beam, like a comm laser. I don't think we can run that risk."

There was another pause, and this time when Lt. Ramirez spoke his voice lacked some of the confidence it had held earlier. "Captain?" he said.

"I agree," he said. There was no hesitation in his voice at all. "Abort the mission."

"Aye, sir." The crispness was back in Ramirez's voice,

as though some of the captain's decisiveness had rubbed off on him.

"How long until your team can regroup, Lieutenant?"

"Five minutes, sir, if there's nothing in the central compartment to delay us."

"That's too long. Forget about regrouping, Lieutenant. Just get all of your people off that ship by the fastest routes available. And don't wait for the pickup. If the pirates spot our shuttle returning to the derelict, they might just go ahead and detonate."

"Aye, sir."

"Mr. Jenkins, maintain your position until I give the word. If there is a bomb on board that ship, I don't want anything to spook the pirates into setting it off before we've gotten our people off."

"Aye, sir," I said, but I didn't like this plan. In order for it to work, the boarding party would have to abandon ship in such a way that the pirates didn't see them leaving—which meant they couldn't stay together in a nice, tight group. Which meant that I would be picking up a dozen different crewmen, with only their suit-based jet packs to help them steer toward my ship, and there was every chance that I'd be doing it while under fire from one or more of the pirate ships.

No, I didn't like this plan at all. I didn't disagree with it, and I certainly didn't have a better suggestion, but I didn't like it at all.

An indicator inside my helmet lit up, telling me to switch to a private channel. When I did, I found the captain and Lieutenant Ramirez there ahead of me.

"Mr. Jenkins," the captain said, "you need to hear this so you know what's going on when you pick up the crew. Lt. Ramirez has some concerns about our chances of getting everyone off that ship before the bomb goes off. I agree, and so I've instructed the lieutenant to remain behind. He will try to find the bomb and to deactivate it before it goes off. As soon as he radios you that the bomb has been neutralized, your highest priority will be recovering the eleven other members of the lieutenant's team. Once they are all safely on board your shuttle you will return to that vessel for the lieutenant, but not before. Is that understood, Mr. Jenkins?"

"Yes, sir."

"Good. I'm breveting you to full Guardsman for the duration of this mission. Good luck, Mr. Jenkins."

"Thank you, sir," I said.

The captain clicked off, leaving Ramirez and me alone on the private channel.

"Jenkins," he said. "I'm counting on you. Those crewmen are my responsibility, and now they're yours, too."

"Don't worry—" I started to say, but he cut me off.

"Shut up," he said. "We don't have much time. I want you to pick up my team as soon as they're off this ship, and I want you to take them back to the *Michelangelo*. Once they're safe you can come back for me, but not before. Is that understood?"

"No, sir," I said. "I mean, yes, sir, but I can't do it. The captain said—"

"The captain said those crewmen are your highest priority. Don't worry about me, Jenkins. Just get them to safety."

"Lieutenant—"

"We're out of time. You have your orders, Mr. Jenkins. Now carry them out."

I sighed. "Yes, sir," I said. "Good luck," I added, but he was already gone, back to the team frequency, issuing orders and starting the evacuation.

My last words echoed in my helmet. *Good luck to us all*, I thought, and then I turned my attention back to my board and to waiting for the signal to act.

Chapter Twenty-Six

The next ten minutes were among the longest of my life. I spent most of them tracking the various ships on my monitor—the three incoming pirate vessels, the two shuttles piloted by Lts. Wu and Freeman, my own runabout, the derelict colony ship, and the *Michelangelo* herself. Both Wu and Freeman had altered their courses slightly, bringing their pickets in closer to the *Michelangelo* without being obvious, but that wouldn't help me or the boarding party at all. Their job was to defend the *Michelangelo*. It was up to me to get Lt. Ramirez and his team home safely.

A few minutes later, Ramirez made his first report. "I've found the comm unit. It's in the central compartment, and it appears to be wired up to a couple of damaged solar panels. No sign of the bomb yet."

I could picture the scene he was describing. That set up had to be intentionally designed to send out an intermittent signal. The damaged panels would charge up enough to send out a partial message, like the one we detected, and then wouldn't be able to send again until they recharged. It would sound just like a ship in genuine distress—perfect bait for a perfect trap. At least, it would have been, if not for Jamie.

"We're clear, Lieutenant." I couldn't tell who was speaking, but it sounded like B Group's leader. "The last crewman has jumped ship."

"Did you copy that, Jenkins?" Ramirez said. "Give them time to get clear of the ship, and then start your pickup run."

The crewmen would use their jet packs to accelerate away from the ship. Not knowing how powerful the bomb was, there was no way to tell what a safe distance was. They simply had to get as far away from the derelict as possible.

My orders were clear. The captain had said that I was to wait for the bomb to be neutralized before making my move, but the lieutenant was right. We were out of time. Every moment that I delayed simply increased the risk that we would lose the entire boarding party. "Aye, sir," I said.

I gave them two minutes and then I hit my jets. The suit packs weren't designed for speed, and I would have liked to have given them longer, but I knew that I didn't have much time. If I was going to have any chance to get the lieutenant off that ship in time, I had to find the right balance of waiting and acting.

I didn't find it. Perhaps there *was* no right balance. Maybe once we'd boarded that ship we'd had no chance of ever returning home safely. Or perhaps it was someone else's fault—like the lieutenant's for offering to defuse the bomb, or the captain's for allowing him to try. I didn't know, couldn't know, exactly what happened, or why it happened, or how it might have happened differently. All I knew was that I hit my jets and that derelict colony vessel went up in a burst of light.

There were no flames, of course. There had been no oxygen on board, nothing to fuel a fire, but that didn't make the damage any less severe.

The lieutenant never had a chance. He'd been looking for one bomb, or a single triggering device, but it was obvious that the pirates had planted more than one.

Two explosions went off simultaneously, one at each end of the ship. The charges must have been shaped in some way, because I could see that most of the force of each blast was funnelled inward, toward the center of the ship. A moment later a third charge went off, right in the very heart of the middle section.

This third charge was not shaped at all. It combined with the force of the first two blasts and blew the central section of the ship apart. I knew in that moment that the lieutenant was dead.

There was a series of smaller explosions, then, in the two remaining outer sections. The drive section and the crew section disintegrated, leaving very little behind.

I sat there, stunned, staring at my screens. The ship had been there, right there, just a heartbeat before, and now it was gone, taking the lieutenant with it.

But I didn't have a chance to think about what had just happened. The afterimages of the explosions were still dancing on my retinas when my radio started to pick up cries of pain from some of the crewmen. Debris from the ship, powered by the force of the simultaneous blasts, was peppering them, ripping through their self-sealing suits and their flesh like shrapnel. The same debris was hitting my ship as well, but with no atmosphere on board I couldn't hear the impacts. I simply had to trust that the armored hull would hold up.

With shaking hands, I turned my ship toward the nearest crewman and started my run.

Chapter Twenty-Seven

It took me nearly ten minutes to recover all eleven crewmen. Under the circumstances, I made good time, but it seemed to take forever. Six of the team members were hurt—three of them badly, including Vasquez—but at that I knew we'd gotten off lucky. They were all still alive, and their suits had managed to seal around the damage. With prompt medical attention it looked like they would all stay alive.

They tended to each other's wounds as best they could while I took us back toward the *Michelangelo*. My job was to fly the ship. The most I could do was to pressurize the cabin so they could remove their suits and treat their injured teammates.

Hanks, the senior member of the team now that the lieutenant was gone and one of the uninjured crewmen, joined me at the controls.

"What's the status?" he asked.

I gestured toward my screens. "I don't know," I said. "It looks like the battle has started, but I can't tell how it's going."

The three pirate ships had started their own runs, with all three darting in toward the *Michelangelo*. Wu and

Freeman had both accelerated to cut off two of the ships, but as far as I could tell no one had fired a shot yet.

"Here," Hanks said, pointing toward one of the ships. "This one is coming in toward the *Michelangelo*. Hang back until the engagement is resolved."

I looked at him, and then looked at the injured team members. "Hang back?" I asked. "But—"

He shook his head. "You don't understand," he said. "The *Michelangelo* won't be able to maneuver if we're trying to dock while she's engaged. We have to let her fight first, and not dock until the battle is over."

"Oh," I said.

"Head toward the *Michelangelo*, but keep your speed slow. We don't want them to know we're expecting a fight, but we don't want to get in the way, either."

I nodded and turned back toward home.

The battle didn't last long. The pirates had obviously been counting on surprise. They came in slowly, trying to hide their presence for as long as possible, and ended up walking right into the countertrap the captain had set for them. Our two shuttles engaged two of the enemy ships before the pirates were ready. Hanks and I watched as Wu and Freeman brought their vessels into position and opened fire. One barrage each and the pirate vessels were gone.

The third enemy ship, the one we'd detected first, launched a single salvo at the *Michelangelo* and then turned to try to run. It was out of distance when it fired, and did no damage, but in turning away from the other two shuttles it headed in our direction.

"Johnson," Hanks said, "man the starboard guns. You're going to get a shot at those bastards. Make it count."

"Aye, sir," Johnson said, leaping to the weapons controls.

"Keep us steady, Pilot," Hanks said. "Johnson may only have the one shot."

My hands grew sweaty once more. Without being able to maneuver, we were an easy target for the oncoming pirate vessel. If they chose to launch at us, there wouldn't be much we could do about it. But Hanks was right. For all we knew, that was the ship that had given the signal to blow their bombs. I didn't want them to get away any more than he did.

"Aye, sir," I said.

This close, I could finally start to make out some details of the enemy craft. It was long and slender, tapering at the bow like a deadly needle. I could see bulges all along its length, devices that were probably sensors and weapons.

We probably should have tried to capture that ship. We could have learned something from it, something about the stealth technology they were employing, and perhaps how to overcome it. But I knew from the look on Hanks' face that we weren't going to try for any disabling shot.

The distance closed quickly at first, but before Johnson could get off a decent shot they changed course, angling away from us instead of drawing closer. They also picked up some speed—not enough to register on our screens, but enough to take them away from us quickly. They had obviously detected us and were trying to stay out of reach of our guns.

At the weapons console, Johnson shook his head. "It's no good, sir," he said. "Our sensors won't lock onto them."

Beside me, Hanks frowned. I knew he wanted to order me to change course to intercept, but I also knew he wouldn't do it. Not with three badly injured crewmen on board, all of whom needed immediate medical attention. I was also pretty sure that Captain Browne would not give chase. One small pirate craft—even one with stealth capabilities—was not as important as our crewmen aboard that alien ship, and every moment we stayed in this system cut our chances of recovering them safely.

"Go to manual mode," Hanks said. "Try and get off a shot at least."

I felt the ship shudder and Johnson fired off the starboard guns, but there was no excitement within me. It was a hopeless shot, I knew, with practically no chance of finding the mark. Without a sensor lock, I couldn't say for sure how far we were from the pirate vessel, but I knew we were far enough to make it a difficult shot. The fact that it was a small ship, that we couldn't get even a minimal read on it, and that it was accelerating away from us all combined to make this a nearly impossible shot.

I glanced at my board long enough to see that he had come closer than I had expected, but he'd still missed.

"Sorry, sir," Johnson said.

Hanks didn't reply immediately. He just watched the screens, his eyes locked on the enemy ship. After a moment he sighed and said, "Nice try, Johnson, but rack the guns. They're out of range."

"Aye, sir."

Turning to me, Hanks said, "Take us home, Pilot."

"Aye, sir," I said, and started making preparations for our final approach.

Chapter Twenty-Eight

There were a lot of cheers and excitement on board the *Michelangelo*, but I didn't take part in any of them. Most of the crew had been able to follow much of the battle on their monitors and knew that we'd avoided a pirate trap and sprung one of our own, taking out two enemy ships in the process. Few of them, however, were aware of the injuries we had sustained, or the fact that Lt. Ramirez had not made it off the colony ship before it blew.

I headed straight to the bridge to make my report and to face the music. I knew what was coming, and I knew that I deserved every bit of it. If I was lucky, the captain would simply have me drummed out of the service, but I expected a full court-martial.

I had disobeyed the captain. For all the right reasons, and under orders from the lieutenant, but that didn't change the fact that I had disobeyed my captain—and that simple fact had led directly to the death of Lt. Ramirez.

The bridge had never seemed so far away. All the other times I'd made this walk I'd been filled with excitement and anticipation. Never again, I knew. I'd killed a man, a crewmate, and I'd never make this walk again. More than that, though, I had the feeling that I'd never find excitement or anticipation in anything ever again.

The expressions that greeted me told me that everyone there knew exactly what had happened, and what my own role in it had been. I walked up to the captain and came to attention, feeling the weight of my own guilt pulling at me. "I'm sorry, sir," I said, snapping off the crispest salute I could. "I moved too soon, and the pirates detonated their bombs before Lt. Ramirez was able to find and neutralize their devices. Six members of the boarding party were injured by debris, three badly. All eleven survivors are currently in sick bay being examined and receiving treatment, but the lieutenant did not survive." The captain knew all this already, but protocol demanded that I make a complete report and I wasn't about to ignore protocol again. "He was unable to make it off the ship before it blew." I took a deep breath before going on. "He's gone, sir, and it's my fault. I stand ready to accept the consequences."

Captain Browne had not moved during my little speech. He merely stood there, his face hard and expressionless, meeting my gaze with his own. When I had finished, he nodded, once, and said, "Apprentice Guardsman Jenkins, you are hereby relieved of duty pending further review." His face softened then, just the slightest bit. "Tom," he said, "this is merely a formality. We lost a good man today, but it *wasn't* your fault. I've reviewed the conversations you had with the lieutenant, and you did the right thing—the only thing you could do under the circumstances. Relieving you of duty is merely a formality until I can call a board to examine the circumstances."

I didn't say anything, but I knew he was wrong. I could have done something different—I *should* have done something different. I just didn't know what, and that was part of the reason that I didn't deserve to wear the uniform. I'd made a mistake. I'd cost another Guardsman his life. And I hadn't learned a thing.

"Dismissed," the captain said.

I saluted again. Spinning on my heel, I left the bridge.

Chapter Twenty-Nine

Jamie found me on my bunk a couple hours later. He came in silently, and stood for a moment, motionless, in the doorway. Then he came over and stood beside my bunk.

"My God, Tom," he said. "I just heard. I'm so sorry."

I was lying on my back, staring up at the gunmetal grey ceiling, and for a long time I didn't answer him. I just couldn't find anything to say.

"You want to talk about it?" he asked.

I pressed my lips together and shook my head.

"Can I get you anything?"

I shook my head again.

"Is there anything at all I can do?"

I could hear the pain in his voice, the desire to help, but no one could help me anymore, not even myself.

Looking at him, I forced a half smile onto my face. "Thanks, Jamie," I said. "I appreciate it, but there's nothing to be done. The captain will call his meeting and I'll be gone. If I'm lucky, they'll let me off at the next port. If not—"

"Don't say that," Jamie said. "This isn't over, Tom. We can fight this thing—"

I shook my head. "No," I said. "We can't. They're right, Jamie. I screwed up, and because of that one crewman is dead and six more are injured. No, my friend. I'm afraid I just don't deserve to wear the blues."

Jamie glared at me, something like anger showing on his face. "Yes, you do," he said. "God dammit, Tom, yes, you do." Spinning on his heel, he stormed out of our bunk room, leaving me to stew and fret alone.

A little while later, I roused enough to cross over to the computer terminal and request a status report on the injured crewmen. Three of them had been treated and released. It looked like they would be off active duty for the next couple of days, but would be fine. Of the other three, two had stabilized and were out of danger, but Vasquez was still listed in critical condition.

I considered heading down to sick bay, but decided against it. No one down there wanted to see me, or hear my apologies.

Shutting down the terminal, I headed out to get some food.

I ended up in the library, a half-eaten sandwich and a cold cup of coffee at my elbow.

The last time I had been here, I was full of excitement and enthusiasm, determined to solve a puzzle before anyone else. Now, though, all I wanted was a distraction, something to lose myself in and to take my mind off the problems I had created.

I no longer had a future, of that I was certain, and so I did the only thing I could think of to do: I went looking, once more, for my past. And I found it—a piece of it, at least.

Among all the reports of lost ships, missing crewmen, and unaccountable disappearances, there were also numerous listings of discoveries, recovered ships, and closed cases. And one of those was me. There, buried

among all the others, was the official report from the
crew who first found my survival pod drifting in space.

I'd seen this report before, as a civilian, but at that
time I hadn't had access to all the details. The version
I'd seen then had been sanitized, with a lot of the
information deleted, and it hadn't occurred to me to go
looking for the original, complete report.

I read it with great interest, memorizing the exact
location where I was found, the vector and speed my
ship was travelling when it was picked up, and many
other details, including a description of the capsule itself.
Vasquez and Hanks had said that there were no pods
left on board that ship we'd come across, so I couldn't
match this description with anything concrete, but from
the sound of it the pod that had carried me could have
come from that ship. The size was right for the bays
they'd found, and the lack of markings matched the
colony ship itself.

I sat back in my chair, rubbing at my face, thinking
about those flashes of visions I'd had earlier. Had I really
been on board that ship? If so, what had happened? How
did I get off, and why did I lose my memory? And what
about the other missing pods? Were there other survivors?
If so, who were they, and where had they gone?

I didn't want to ask these questions. I would never
have the chance to answer them. Not sitting at a computer keyboard. No, the only way to answer even one
of these questions was to track down the other pods, or
capture one of the pirates who'd been involved in the
taking of that colony ship, or to find another survivor,
somehow, somewhere. And the only way I would ever
be able to do any of that was on board a Space Guard
vessel, as a member of her crew.

And that would never happen. Not now. Not after
what I had done.

Before me, the computer screen blurred as hot, bitter
tears stung at my eyes.

It was suddenly just all too much for me. Pushing back from the terminal, I rose to my feet, not even bothering to save the results of my search or power down the machine.

I had to get away. With nowhere else to go, I headed back to my room, hoping that Jamie wasn't there and that I could be alone to sulk, to mourn, and to cry.

Chapter Thirty

I spent much of the next two days poring over the images shot by various members of the boarding party. I spent hours reviewing the layout of that ship, studying the look of the corridors, the texture of the flooring, looking for anything that would seem familiar or might trigger another vision. But nothing did. All I got for my effort was a pounding headache and a feeling of failure and frustration.

On the third day we rendezvoused with Alex and Ensign Davies and brought the shuttle on board once more. Part of me wanted to be there when they emerged from their long stay in the shuttle, but I didn't dare head down to the hangar bay. I was persona non grata, and had no place anywhere on board this ship. So, instead, I stayed in my room throughout the maneuvers, listening to the exchanges through the computer.

I did try to pipe in a visual feed, however. I wanted to see them as they came out of the shuttle, to be able to read their body language, to see how close they stood to each other and how often they touched. I no longer even dared to dream that Alex could one day be mine. My own actions had cut me off from any sort of future with the Guard, and with Alex. Still, I had to know just what had happened on board that shuttle.

But I couldn't. They had uploaded their reports directly to the bridge as soon as we had come within range, and both Alex and Ensign Davies had already spoken with the captain, and so there was no ceremony to greet them and no visual link for me to hook into.

I could picture them in my mind's eye: both of them disheveled and in need of a shower. It was easy to imagine her turning to him, a soft look in her eyes, thanking him for helping her. I could see him reach out and touch her face, and the smile she gave him in return.

My hands clenching into sudden fists, I switched the computer off and rose to my feet. I had no idea what I was going to do, and before I could figure it out the door slid open and Jamie came in.

He took one look at my face and stopped. "My God, Tom," he said. "Are you all right? What happened?"

I turned away. "Nothing, Jamie," I said, my voice as ragged as my emotions. "What's up?"

I heard him take another couple of steps into the room and turn the computer on again. "You sure you're all right?"

Yeah, I thought. *I'm just great, Jamie. I have no purpose, no future, and no chance with Alex, but beyond that everything's fine.*

I didn't say that, though. He was my friend, and he was trying to help, and I did appreciate that.

Slowly I turned to face him. "I'm fine, Jamie," I said. "Thanks. Now what's up?"

"The captain's asking for a final opinion on which way to go. I'd like your help, Tom."

I shook my head. "Not me, my friend," I said, and even I could hear the bitterness in my voice. "I can't be any help to anyone anymore, I'm afraid."

Jamie reached out and caught my arm. "Dammit, Tom," he said, his face suddenly harsher than I'd ever seen it. "How long are you going to do this to yourself? How long are you going to wallow in your own self-pity?"

I stiffened, and started to pull away, but he wouldn't let me.

"This is more important than just you, you know," he went on, his voice hard and relentless. "We've got three missing crewmen. We're on the verge of what could be the greatest discovery since space flight itself. And like it or not, you're a part of that, and it's time for you to get back to work. Now."

I looked at him, and for a moment I didn't know whether to get mad at him or break down and cry.

"I can't, Jamie," I said, and this time all I heard in my voice was defeat and despair.

"Yes, Tom," he said. "You can."

I sighed then and turned to look at the computer. "All right," I said. "I'll try. Show me what you've got."

Jamie spun to face the computer, turning too quickly for me to get a good look at his face, but I thought I caught a glimpse of something that looked like triumph. I clapped him on the shoulder, and then gave my full attention to the images he'd called up on the screen.

"All right," he said. "This is the enhanced sensor data of the alien ship as it disappeared. We've looked at that stretching motion from every angle. We've run computer simulation after computer simulation, trying to understand exactly what we're seeing."

I glanced at him. "And have you figured it out?"

He frowned and shook his head. "No," he said. "We've got some guesses, but no solid answers."

I nodded. No one could have expected miracles from them, after all. "What are your guesses?"

He pointed at the screen. "What we think is happening is that this ship is employing a translation technique. You know the theory of wormholes, right?"

"Sure," I said. "Holes in space—or, more accurately, holes through the warp and weave of space that cut across another dimension. As I understand it, the easiest way to visualize it is to think of a piece of paper. Make a drawing of a star system on one side of the paper, and draw a second system on the other side. That's space. To get from the center of one system to the center of the other, you can either draw a line to the edge of the paper, wrap around, and then continue your line—which is how we do it today—or you can punch a hole right through the paper. That's a wormhole. Or at least, that's the theory."

He nodded. "You did pay attention in Mr. Forrester's class, didn't you?"

I shrugged. "Sometimes."

He grinned, then grew serious again. "Okay. So that's what we think they're doing. We think that this ship punched a hole through space itself, a hole with one side here, in the system where we found it, and the other . . . somewhere else."

"Yeah," I said. "But where?"

"That's what we're trying to figure out—and here's where it gets tricky. You see, if we're right about the wormhole idea, and if we understand the theory behind it as well as we think we do, then there is no actual, physical travel, at least not in our universe. I mean, you don't just create this hole out there off your port bow and then drive your ship through it. Instead, there's a sort of internal movement, a translation from a three-dimensional solid to a one-dimensional object that can pass freely through the very fabric of space. We think."

I paused, trying to think that one through, but my mind kept balking at the idea of translating from three dimensions to one dimension. We were three-dimensional objects ourselves. We had height, length, and width. Planes were two-dimensional. They had no height, only length and width, but the only planes we'd ever discovered were in textbooks. So what had only one dimension? A point?

No, I thought. *Not a point. A line.* It had infinite length, but no height and no width.

Which made sense, I realized. A single dimensional line could pass through the very fabric of our space. If there was a way to translate back to three dimensions at any point along that line, you could theoretically translate from one point in space to another anywhere along that line, without ever actually moving.

But how? How would something like that work? And what would it feel like to translate from three dimensions to one or two?

After a few moments I said, "I don't get it, Jamie. I can't see how such a thing might be done."

He grinned at me. "To be honest, Tom, I don't either, but the brains on board seem to think they're on to something. They're all excited about this, anyway. See, if they're right, then they don't have to go out and find already existing wormholes, or wormholes that have physical openings into our universe. If they're right, wormholes aren't necessary at all. Instead, all you need to do is figure out how to perform this translation. Travel from point to point becomes instantaneous, with no acceleration or deceleration. Which means that if they're right, and if we can master this technology, it will be possible for us to travel anywhere in the universe in an instant. Think of that, Tom. Think of the possibilities."

I shook my head. I didn't want to think of that. Not now. It was simply too much, too fast, for me to take in.

"All right," I said. "So we think they're translating themselves through the very fabric of space, and we're assuming that the stretching we're seeing represents the vector of this translation." He nodded. "So where does it go? If we extend the lines, which systems do they intersect?"

Jamie shrugged, his enthusiasm fading as he returned to the matter at hand. "In theory, an infinite number," he said. "Remember, distance is irrelevant—except we're assuming it isn't. We're assuming that it takes a finite amount of energy to create this translation, and we're hoping that the amount of power is a function of the length of the single dimensional line."

I frowned at that. "How confident are they of that?"

He shrugged again. "I don't know, but we're taking it as a working assumption."

"Why?"

"Because otherwise we have no chance of recovering our crewmen."

"Oh," I said, feeling suddenly very stupid. He was right, of course. If the executive officer and the other two were three billion light years away right now, we would never see them again. "All right, then what systems intersect within a reasonable distance?"

"Well," Jamie said, "there's actually one more question we have to consider. Remember, Tom, we're talking now about points in space, a single, one-dimensional line cutting through the very fabric of the space-time continuum. It's not the same thing as pointing a ship at a star and hitting the jets, or even jumping into hyperspace."

I nodded, but I didn't see his point.

"See, Tom, we have to take into account how long that ship has been there. Remember, planetary systems aren't motionless in space. Our entire galaxy is moving. It's rotating—slowly, but perceptibly—and it's also moving outward. Which means that if that ship has sat there long enough, and if it hasn't been able to keep track of time and the motion of the stars, it may have jumped to empty space."

I thought about that. "You mean it might have jumped to a spot where a system was eons ago, but that system would have moved on by now."

"Exactly. Depending on how long that ship has been there, its target system may be light years away by now."

"So how do we know?" I asked. "How do we determine how long it's been there?"

Jamie sighed. "We don't. They've gone over every bit of data squeezed out of the sensor records, and there's just no way to pin down the age of that ship. They believe that it is very old, but that's as far as they can narrow it down."

"That's not very helpful."

"I know. But that's what we have to work with."

I nodded. "All right. Can you give me a dynamic view of this region? Overlay the motion of the systems for the past few million years? Maybe we'll see something."

Jamie worked the controls. He called up a schematic of this region of space, centered on the spot where we'd discovered the ship. He also laid in a purple line showing the two directions the ship might have gone. The purple line extended up and down to the edges of the monitor, both halves pointing away from the travel lanes and out into unfamiliar territory. Then he put the stars in motion, tracing in reverse the paths they had taken in the short time mankind had been around.

Nothing really jumped out at me, though. There were several systems that intersected each half of the purple line, but without a referent, without a guess as to how far back to go, there was just no way to know.

After a moment I shook my head. "I think this is wrong," I said.

He looked at me. "Why?" he asked.

"Two reasons. First, I just don't believe it. That ship detected our presence immediately. You saw the visuals. There was no detectable time between when the remote unit entered that ship and the whole thing disappeared. That tells me that there was some sensing device active the whole time. And if that's the case, I have to believe there was some navigation device active, too. It just wouldn't make sense otherwise."

Jamie looked unconvinced. "I don't know, Tom," he

said. "After all, we're talking aliens here. I don't think you can be sure of what makes sense and what doesn't."

"We have to make some assumptions, buddy," I said. "Otherwise we're just guessing."

He nodded. "You said two reasons. What's the second?"

"What you said earlier. Without pinning down a time frame, we have no chance of narrowing down which of these old locations it might have jumped to—which means we have no chance of determining where it might have gone. And that, my friend, means that we have no chance of recovering our missing crewmen."

"All right," he said. "You've convinced me. Which brings us back to where we started." He stopped the motion on the screen, returning the stars to their present configuration. "In this direction," he said, pointing toward the top of the screen, "the vector doesn't intersect any systems directly, at least not within the range we've selected, but it does pass very close to two different multiple planet systems, either of which may have been capable of supporting life once. In the other direction," he pointed down toward the bottom edge of the screen, "there is a system directly along the path. The problem is that this is one of the systems that hasn't been fully charted yet. We don't know if it's even capable of supporting life. So," he said, turning to face me once more, "what's your best guess?"

"That one," I said, pointing toward the bottom of the screen.

"Really? I was thinking these." He pointed to the two systems along the top half of the purple line. "After all, with two nearby star systems, it doubles our chances that the ship was heading toward one of them."

I shook my head. "I don't think so, Jamie. Why would a ship with jump technology only go close to a system? It doesn't make sense."

"But—"

"I know," I said, cutting him off. "We're talking about aliens, but like I said, Jamie, if we can't make some assumptions then the whole thing is hopeless, right?"

He nodded.

"All right. So let's assume they were going somewhere specific. That means this system here, or else one we couldn't get to in time."

Jamie looked at me, then at the screen, and then back at me. Finally he nodded. "All right, Tom," he said. "I agree. The final decision is up to the captain, of course, but he's asked for recommendations, and that's what I'll tell him. I just hope to God that he picks the right direction, whichever one that is."

I nodded. "Me, too, my friend," I said. "Let me know what he decides, okay?"

"Of course." Jamie turned and started to leave, but he paused at the door and turned back for a moment. "Thanks, Tom," he said, and then he was gone.

I stood there for a time, staring at the monitor. I suspected that the captain wasn't going to place a whole lot of confidence in our reasoning. He had so many smarter, wiser, and more experienced people on board that I was pretty sure Jamie had come down here mostly to make me feel better. And it had worked. For one brief, shining moment I was a part of this crew again, and it had felt great.

I glanced over at the empty doorway. "Thanks, Jamie," I said.

Sitting down once more, I cleared the screen and called up the visuals from the colony ship. I had work to do.

Chapter Thirty-One

There was a memorial service for Lt. Ramirez later. I hadn't planned on attending. I told myself that it just didn't seem proper for the man responsible for his death to show up at his funeral, but that was a lie. The truth was that I simply didn't want to go. I didn't want to face the rest of the crew. I didn't want to see their faces when they looked at me.

But I went. I never really made a conscious decision to go, but as the time drew nearer I found myself putting on my dress whites and heading down to the little auditorium that served as a meeting place whenever most of the crew needed to assemble.

The room was dark when I arrived. The stage itself, a small dais at the front of the room, was brightly lit, with a single spot focussed on the podium, but the rest of the room was in shadow. There was just enough light for me to see that most of the crew was gathered, and that many of them had worn their dress uniforms. Those that weren't there were probably still on duty.

Jamie was also there, seated toward the back, and I was making my way over to him when I felt a light touch upon my arm.

"Tom."

I turned and saw Alex sitting with Ensign Davies. I had walked right in front of them without even seeing them.

The sight was like a blow, unexpected and devastating, and for a moment I couldn't breathe.

"Tom," she said, her voice low and urgent. "I heard what happened. We need to talk."

I glanced over at Ensign Davies. He was looking at me silently, an earnest expression on his face. Looking back at Alex I shook my head. "Thanks," I said, "but things are pretty hectic right now. Maybe later."

"No, Tom." Her hand slid down my arm and caught at my hand. "We need to talk soon. Meet me in the lounge when this is over. Please, Tom. It's important."

Her other hand was resting lightly on her thigh. Davies' hand was lying next to hers, on his own leg. I couldn't tell if they'd been holding hands or not, but I suspected they had been.

I had been trying to resign myself to this. I knew what must have happened on board that shuttle while we were away chasing pirates. I knew that whatever I'd hoped might happen between Alex and myself had gone away, and I was pretty sure that was what she wanted to talk about. She had to know how I felt, and she was not the kind of person to leave me hanging—not once she'd made up her mind. But I just didn't have the strength to hear it. Not now, and maybe not ever.

I shook my head. "I can't," I said. "Maybe some other time." And then I pushed past them. I didn't look back.

"Wow," Jamie said when I dropped into the seat beside him. "What was all that about?"

"I don't know, Jamie," I said. "I honestly don't know."

"Well, I'm glad to see you came. I wasn't sure you would."

"I wasn't sure either, but I had to come."

He nodded.

"So," I said, changing the subject, "what did the captain decide?"

Jamie grinned at me. "He agreed with you," he said. I just looked at him, and after a moment he added, "Well, all right, a few others had come up with some of your same points—"

And a few I missed, I'm sure, I thought.

"—but what matters is that the captain came to the same conclusion you did. We're currently making top speed toward that single star system."

I nodded. "What's our ETA?"

Jamie sobered a bit at that. "Thirteen days."

I grunted. "Ouch," I said. "They'll be dead by then, won't they?"

He nodded slowly. "Unless a miracle happens. The captain has left Lt. Wu behind in a shuttle. He's hoping the alien ship will return, and wants to have someone on station to recover our crewmen if that happens."

I didn't say anything to that. We both knew that was clutching at straws, but we also knew we had nothing else to clutch at.

The captain came in then, resplendent in his white uniform, medals gleaming among the ribbons on his chest. The room fell silent as Captain Browne strode up to the podium and began speaking.

"There are three tasks that occasionally fall to the captain of a vessel such as ours, three tasks that we hate and fear more than any others. This is one of those tasks: calling the crew together to mourn the passing of one of our own."

He looked around the auditorium. He couldn't have seen much, not with the spotlight shining full upon him and the rest of the room in darkness, but it seemed that he made eye contact with each and every one of us seated among the shadows.

"Enrigo Ramirez was a good man and a good officer. Full of ambition—he told me once that he expected to make full captain by the time he was thirty. He was also full of compassion and concern for those crewmen who were placed in his care. Nothing could demonstrate that better than the way he died, sacrificing his life in an effort to protect his team."

Captain Browne leaned forward, resting his forearms on the podium in front of him. His medals caught the light from the spot. Breaking into dozens of pieces, the reflections cast out among the audience, touching different crewmen as his chest rose and fell in time with his speaking.

"But Enrigo Ramirez was more than a good man and a good officer. He was, as all of you are, a good Guardsman. He understood the traditions and the responsibilities that he put on along with that uniform. He knew the sacrifice he might someday be called on to make, and he understood the reasons why it might one day be necessary for him to give his life. The Space Guard is a thin blue line, weaving its way among the stars and forming the last, best defense of mankind against the forces of anarchy and chaos. Lt. Enrigo Ramirez gave his life in that defense, as each and every one of us gathered here today would give our lives, if necessary."

I thought about that for a moment and realized that he was right. I believed that everyone in that audience, Jamie and myself included, would carry out our duties as necessary regardless of the cost. It made me feel a bit better to know that about myself.

"Enrigo Ramirez was a good man, a good officer, and a good Guardsman. May he rest in peace, and may God have mercy upon his soul."

At his last word, the spotlight faded and went out. From out of the darkness, piped in through the computers no doubt, came the sound of a lone trumpet playing a dirge. When the song ended, the lights came up and, once the captain had departed, the assembled crew started filing out.

"Wow," Jamie said, rising to his feet. "That must have been tough. I can see why that would be one of the hardest tasks a captain can face. I wonder what the other two are."

"Telling the family, I would guess," I said. "I mean, it's one thing to stand up in front of a group of Guardsmen and talk about sacrifice and tradition. It's something else to tell that to people who don't understand what it means to be a Guardsman."

"Good guess, Mr. Jenkins," said a new voice from behind me. I turned and saw Lt. O'Malley standing there. "The third task, and the one that's the hardest, is sending a member of your crew on a dangerous mission, one that you know will put him in harm's way. For a good officer—and Captain Browne is one of the best—ordering a man to his death is unimaginably more difficult than going to your own."

His eyes locked on mine. "But there are lots of difficult tasks for Guardsmen," he said. "Attending a friend's funeral, or standing by, helpless, watching a crewmate die. It can tear you up inside, make you second-guess yourself, make you question your fitness as a Guardsman, and knowing that others have gone through it doesn't make it any easier, I know."

He took a deep breath, his eyes still locked on mine. "It wasn't your fault, Tom," he said. "What happened out there wasn't your fault."

I shook my head. "Yes," I said. "It was. Not just because I was there, and not just because I was charged with getting the team home safely, but because I was too slow. I was too slow to realize the nature of the trap and too slow pulling them out. It *was* my fault. Lt. Ramirez should not have died, not on that ship and not on that mission. If I'd been faster, he'd still be alive."

"That's not true." I held up a hand to stop him but he kept on, relentlessly. "You don't understand. I *wanted* to blame you for this. Rigo was a friend of mine and I wanted to be able to blame his death on a punk apprentice from Brighthome. I've spent hours going over the records of what happened, trying to figure out where the mission went wrong, and I'm telling you that what happened wasn't your fault. Sometimes there is no fault. Sometimes you do everything right, by the book, and still people die. It happens. As the captain said, it's part of being a Guardsman."

I shook my head. "I'd like to believe you," I said, "but I was there. I know the truth, and what happened to Lt. Ramirez is not just a part of being a Guardsman. Mistakes aren't part of our tradition. I made one, maybe two, and cost a man his life. There's no other way to see it."

Lt. O'Malley started to say something more but I didn't let him.

"Thanks, Lieutenant," I said. "I appreciate what you're trying to do, but you're wrong. Believe me."

Without waiting for him to reply, I turned and started making my way once more through the now empty seats.

Chapter Thirty-Two

I spent the next couple of days at the workstation in my wardroom. I had seen so many hours of scenes from that colony ship that I felt I could have built a model of it in my sleep. I was even dreaming about it at night— which was exactly what I wanted. I was hoping to find some way to break through whatever barrier had risen to wall off my memories, and in the past four years that ship had been the only thing to find even the smallest of cracks.

It didn't work, however. At the end of the two days I'd had no further images, no visions, no memories, nothing, and a deep sense of frustration was welling up within me.

"I don't get it," I said, leaning back in my chair.

Jamie was on his bunk, studying schematics on a portable reader. "Give it time, Tom," he said. "You're trying to force something that obviously doesn't want to be forced." He sat up, laying his reader aside. "Look at it this way: you went four years with nothing, not a single clue as to who you were or what had happened to you. Now you've had a breakthrough—a small one, perhaps, but still the first real progress you've ever shown. Give it time. Let it happen. The memories will come when they're ready."

I shook my head. "I can't wait that long, my friend. You don't know what it's like. For four years I've dealt with this, always pushing it to the back of my mind because there was no hope, no therapy, no treatment that would give me back what I have lost. I've learned to accept it because I had to. But now, Jamie, now I have hope again, and hope can be a terrible thing. I'm close, Jamie, I know I am. I can feel it. And I can't give up again. I just can't."

Jamie stood up and started to pace. "All right," he said. "Tell me what you know so far, and what you suspect."

I sighed, rubbing at my eyes. "There's not much to tell," I said. "That's the problem."

"Tell me anyway. Maybe talking it through will help."

I nodded. "All right. I know I was on that ship."

Jamie interrupted me. "No, you don't," he said. "You have memories that indicate you were on a ship *like* that one. You don't know that was the ship."

I shrugged. "You're right, but I'm sure it was that one. What are the odds of two similarly configured colony ships being hit by pirates in this same general region of space?"

He stopped pacing. "Pretty good, actually," he said, turning to face me. "Think about it, Tom. This is a good region for colony ships to travel through. It's not heavily patrolled, which gives them a good chance of avoiding the Guard, and yet it's been charted just well enough that they can find suitable destinations. Also, since the Guard doesn't have a real presence here, it's a good place for the pirates to hang out. So the odds are really pretty good that a higher number of colony ships would travel through here, and that more than one of them would run into pirates. In fact, Tom, if you think about it, very few renegade colonies are ever heard from again. Why?"

"That's easy," I said. "Most of them simply don't want

to be part of our society, which is why they left to form their own colonies in the first place—and why they sneaked off to do it in secret. We don't hear from them again because they don't want to talk to us."

"Maybe," he said, starting to pace again, "but maybe most of them run into pirates. After all, they'd be the perfect targets. No one would report them missing, and so the Guard would never come looking for them."

I thought about that. "You're right," I said, "though it's a really depressing thought."

He paused again. "Why?"

"Think about it. These people band together out of a common desire. There's something about today's society that they don't like, or something that's missing, and so they decide to head out among the stars and form their own world, their own version of paradise. They've already rejected our society, however, and, not wanting to take that same society along with them, they seek to avoid official notice. Rather than filing whatever permits are necessary to found a sanctioned colony, they pool their resources and do whatever it takes to acquire their own ship, their own crew, and all the supplies they'll need to make a new start. They pore over the star charts, searching for the perfect destination. Then, full of hope and enthusiasm, they set out . . . only to run into pirates. It's depressing."

"Yeah," he said. "It is. I never thought about it like that."

"I didn't either. Not until just now. But you know, Jamie, I've been thinking about colonists a lot ever since we ran into that ship. I'm thinking now that since my days as a Guardsman are over, maybe I'll sign up with a colony some day—an official one, though. I believe I was already part of an unsanctioned attempt, and that one didn't turn out too well."

He stiffened at my words, his hands balling into tight little fists at his sides. "Tom," he said, his voice low and tight. "Will you quit saying that? Your days as a Guardsman are *not* over. The lieutenant was right—"

"Jamie," I said, cutting him off. "Please. I know what you're trying to do, but trust me on this. I know what I'm talking about. I know what happened out there. I know what I deserve, and what the consequences will be."

"You'll see," he said. "The captain's board will—"

"—Will bear out everything I've said. It's the only possible outcome."

He shook his head, and I was surprised to see the faint glint of tears in his eyes. "You're wrong, Tom," he said. "Dead wrong."

I sighed. "I wish I was, Jamie. But I'm not. I know I'm not."

Jamie opened his mouth again, but he never got the chance to say whatever was on his mind. Before he could speak, the workstation chimed and we both turned to look at it.

"My God," Jamie said. "Look at that."

We still had it set up to monitor the bridge communications, something the captain probably wouldn't have approved of if he'd known, and we watched as a signal came in from Lt. Wu.

"The ship," Jamie said.

"It came back," I said, finishing his thought for him.

"But to a different place." He pointed to the screen as more information scrolled across it. "Look. She says she picked it up on her scopes, but it was nowhere near where we found it the first time."

I nodded. "I see that," I said. "So she left her station and went to investigate it."

"And when she got there, she found no sign of the crewmen." He turned to look at me. "What does that mean?" he asked. "Where are they?"

But I could only shake my head. "I don't know," I said. "But I think we'd better find them."

I pointed to the timer at the bottom corner of the screen. It hadn't reached zero yet, but it was clear that we were rapidly running out of time.

"My God," Jamie said again. "What do you think the captain will do?"

I glanced over at him. "What do you mean?"

"Do you think he'll turn the ship around or keep on this heading?"

That was a good question. "I don't know," I said. "The only reason to go back is to see if that ship itself holds any clues as to where the executive officer and the others are. On the other hand, it would take long enough that even if we figured it out immediately as soon as we got back, it would be too late."

"On the other hand," Jamie said, "if we keep going in this direction, and it's the wrong direction . . ."

I nodded. "Yeah, but we've been through that already. I don't think the captain can afford to second-guess himself now."

The monitor chimed again.

"Hey," Jamie said, "another signal from Lt. Wu." He took the controls from me, calling up more detail on this latest message. "Well," he said, "looks like I've got to get back to work."

"Why?" I asked. "What is it?"

"She sent us her sensor records of the ship's appearance. We'll have to analyze it again, looking for signs of that stretching, and to see if we can learn anything more about where it's been."

"Good luck," I said.

"Thanks, Tom. I have the feeling we'll need it."

Chapter Thirty-Three

The captain didn't turn the ship. He kept us on course, following our best guess as to where the X.O. and the others had gone. With the countdown continuing, and drawing ever closer to zero, the atmosphere on board grew very tense. We were all hoping that the captain had guessed correctly, but I was even more interested in what Jamie had discovered.

"It's a different vector," he said. We were in the cafeteria, sharing a table and grabbing a quick bite. We had the place to ourselves, which was good. This was our first chance to talk since the signals had come in from Lt. Wu.

I looked at him, all sense of hunger disappearing. "What do you mean, a different vector?" I asked.

"The stretching," he said around a mouthful of the sandwich he'd built for himself. He chewed and swallowed, washing it down with a drink of water. "I told you that we'd be looking for signs of it, right?"

I nodded.

"Well, we found it. It wasn't hard to spot, now that we know what to look for, though you still can't see it without the enhancements."

176

"Great," I said. "But what about the vector?"

"It's clear," he said. "It's unmistakable. And it's definitely not the same as the first one. It's in the same plane as the first line we saw, but the angular difference is approximately thirty point one six six degrees."

I stared at him, thinking furiously. "What does it mean?"

He shrugged. "Either all our guesses about the stretching are wrong, or that alien ship returned from somewhere else—somewhere other than where it first went to."

"Why would it do that?"

Jamie shook his head. "If we could even come up with a good guess about that, we'd be a lot further along than we are. The truth is, Tom, that we just have no idea what we're dealing with here."

"But if there's more than one place involved, then we have no hope of finding them in time, do we? I mean, if we assume that ship jumped to only two places before returning to where Lt. Wu is, that still doubles the places where our people could be. We have no hope of reaching both spots before their oxygen runs out."

"I know," he said. Glancing down, he pushed his plate aside, leaving more than half his sandwich untouched. "There is another possibility, though. This could be a different ship."

I frowned and shook my head. "Maybe," I said, "but I don't think so. I mean, we've spent all this time out here among the stars, and we've never found a trace of an alien civilization. What are the odds of finding two different ships, both still functional, within such a short period of time?"

"I don't know," he said, "but maybe it's not that unreasonable. After all, we have no idea what that first ship was doing there. Maybe it wasn't a derelict at all, and maybe that region of space is a regular stopping point."

"A regular stopping point?" I repeated. "What do you mean?"

He shrugged. "I don't know, Tom. I'm just tossing out ideas."

I nodded, but I was no longer really listening to him. I was thinking about what he'd said, trying to make sense of it. "Why would it be a regular stopping point?" I said the words aloud, but I was talking more to myself than to Jamie. "Could this be a patrol ship of some sort?"

"Sure," Jamie said. "Or a scout ship—in which case it is possible that there are more than one."

"A scout ship. Which would mean that the aliens are still alive, still out there somewhere, maybe waiting for someone—us—to follow one of their ships."

Jamie looked at me sharply. "You mean—?"

I nodded. "We may be heading into another trap. Only this time, *we'll* be the ones outgunned."

He paled slightly. "You'd better tell the captain, Tom."

But I shook my head. "No, Jamie," I said. "*You'd* better tell the captain. I don't think he's ready to listen to me."

Jamie frowned at me. "I think you're underestimating the captain, Tom."

"Maybe," I said, "but this is too important to risk it. To be honest, I don't think it will make any difference. Trap or no trap, we still have to make the effort to find out what happened to Lt. Commander Murdoch and the others, but at least this way we'll go in with our guard up."

Jamie nodded, but still he hesitated. "Tom—" he started, but I cut him off.

"Go," I said. "Tell the captain, and let me know what he says. I'll head back to our quarters and work on this some more."

Jamie nodded again, and after one last hard look he turned and left.

I wasted no time. Clearing our plates, I raced back

to our wardroom, turned on the computer, and called up a diagram of this quadrant. Marking off the alien ship's new location, I laid in the two stretch lines Jamie had found and started studying them. They had to make sense. Logic was logic, alien or otherwise, and there had to be meaning to those lines.

As I worked, though, I found myself rethinking what Jamie had said.

A *scout ship*, I thought. To think that the aliens might still be alive, that they might be out there waiting . . . It was incredible. Simply incredible.

But there was a downside to it, I realized. We had been hoping for years—centuries, really—that we would one day discover a companion species out here among the stars. Underlying that hope, however, was the belief that any civilization sophisticated enough to reach for other worlds would have to be peaceful. Space was a frontier that we humans—warlike by nature, violent throughout history—had found we could not conquer as individuals. Historically, several different countries had made it to Earth's moon and the nearest planets, but even exploration of the rest of the solar system had required the cooperation of most of the nations on Earth. And ours had been a united planet for decades before we were able to mount our first manned expedition beyond the limits of our solar system.

We certainly weren't perfect—as the presence of pirates and renegade colonies showed, but we were, for the most part, peaceful. And it was easy to assume that ours was a pattern all civilizations would follow. It took a certain amount of inherent violence, of competition, to drive a race to evolve in the first place. But it took more than that to reach for the stars.

But what if that was wrong? What if some other race had found a way—perhaps by discovering this jump technology before they had matured as a race? What if there was a race of warriors and conquerors who had laid claim to this region, and who were even now waiting for us to find them?

It was a frightening thought. Worse, there was nothing I could do about it. We couldn't turn our backs on our missing crewmen, and we certainly couldn't stop sending our ships out to explore new reaches of space. If there were others out there we would find them, eventually, and if they weren't peaceful . . . Well, we would do whatever we had to do.

Turning my attention back to the monitor and the star charts I'd called up, I saw the timer flashing steadily in the lower right corner of the screen, a constant reminder that I didn't have time to worry about larger issues. Putting those thoughts out of my head, I got back to work.

Chapter Thirty-Four

I couldn't stop thinking about the aliens.

I fought it for a couple of hours, trying to keep working on the star charts and then, unable to concentrate any longer, I headed down to the library to check on some things. I could have accessed the same data from the terminal in my wardroom, but I'd been there too much lately. I needed to get away, and the library seemed like the perfect place to go.

Until Alex came in.

I'd been there maybe half an hour, long enough to make a good start on answering my questions, when I heard the door open and Alex walked in.

"I thought I'd find you here sooner or later," she said. "We need to talk."

I sighed. "No, Alex," I said. I tried to keep the pain out of my voice, but from the look on her face I didn't do a very good job.

"Yes, Tom," she said. Grabbing a cup of coffee from the dispensers, she brought it over and sat down at the carrel next to me.

"Alex," I said, turning to face her, "we don't have time for this. I'm working on something," I indicated the

181

computer screen with my latest search results, "and I need to keep on it."

She glanced at the screen and then turned back to look at me. "Tom," she said, reaching out and placing her hands on mine.

"No," I said. Pulling my hands away, I turned back to the computer.

"It wasn't your fault," she said.

I sighed again. "Yes, it was." I turned back to her once more. "What was it that you said to me, Alex? That I didn't know what it was like to have the lives of others in my hands, and to watch them die? You were right. I didn't. Well, now I do know, and I wish to God I didn't."

"Tom," she said, laying her hands on mine once more. "Tom, I'm sorry. I shouldn't have said that, but you have to understand, I was feeling much the same as you're feeling now: sorry for myself, sorry for those men I was responsible for, and, most of all, feeling guilty as hell. But I shouldn't have taken it out on my friends—and you shouldn't either."

"I'm not," I said. "At least, I hope I'm not. But that doesn't change the fact that Lt. Ramirez's death was my fault—not just because I was the pilot, and not just because I was responsible for bringing them all home safely, but because I made a mistake. I should have figured things out sooner. The pieces were all there, and if I had just put them together in time Lt. Ramirez would still be alive."

Alex touched my cheek very gently. "No, Tom," she said. "He wouldn't."

I looked at her, my work on the computer utterly forgotten. "What do you mean?" I asked.

She picked up her coffee and sat back in her chair. "First of all," she said after taking a sip, "you have to realize that it *wasn't* your fault—or at least it wasn't your fault alone. Those pieces of the puzzle you were talking about, they were right there for everyone to see, including Captain Browne and Lieutenant Ramirez himself. You were the only one to put them together, Tom, the only one to figure it all out."

"Yeah, but too late," I said.

She shook her head. "No," she said. "You saved the lives of the rest of the boarding party."

"But not the lieutenant."

"No," she said again. "No one could have saved him. Don't you see, Tom? You couldn't have figured it out in time. No one could have. You didn't have all the pieces until they had boarded the ship and found the comm unit gone from the bridge—and once they'd boarded the ship, it was already too late. Unless, of course, the lieutenant had left with the others—but he didn't, and that certainly wasn't your fault."

She set her cup down and reached for me once more. "Don't you see, Tom? You would have had to be psychic to recognize that trap before the boarding party entered that ship, and not even you can blame yourself for that."

"No," I said, my voice barely above a whisper. Was she right? I wanted to believe her, but I was honest enough with myself to know that there was also a part of me that *didn't* want to believe her. "I don't know," I said after a moment.

"I understand," she said softly. "But think about it, okay?"

I nodded.

"Now," she said, her voice strengthening once more, "what is it that you're working on?"

I told her. I was still distracted by what she'd said and may not have been as clear and concise as I'd have liked, but she got the picture.

"So you think they might still be alive?" she asked when I had finished.

I shrugged. "I'm not sure, but I think we have to explore the possibility. I mean, I'd rather do the research now and not walk into a trap later."

She nodded, but didn't seem convinced. "True, but I have to say I think it's a waste of time. You saw that ship, Tom. It was *old*. I'm sure that whoever put it there is long gone."

"And yet it still worked," I said. "If their machines could last that long, intact and fully functional, why not the rest of their civilization?"

She frowned and didn't answer. After a moment she gestured toward the monitor and said, "All right, so what are you looking for here?"

"Them," I said. "The aliens. I'm looking for some sign that we've come across them before."

Alex glanced at the screen and then back at me. "Tom," she said, "that doesn't make sense. If we had encountered an alien civilization—or even a world with the ruins of an alien civilization—we would know it. That would be big news, trumpeted across all the worlds. It wouldn't be buried in the Space Guard files, waiting for someone to dig it out."

"No," I said. "That's not what I mean. Obviously, you're right, but that's not what I'm looking for."

She frowned. "Then what *are* you looking for, Tom?"

"Disappearances," I said. "And not just of manned missions, either. I've set the computer to search all records for any probes or expeditions sent out into this region of space. I want a listing of all the ones that went unaccountably silent, and I want the computer to correlate them, looking for anything in common. Is there a pattern, a single system or a finite region of space where most of what we sent out disappeared? If so, that may be evidence of an alien presence."

"Good point," she said. "So, what have you found?"

I sighed. "Nothing. Oh, there have been any number of disappearances, but they don't correlate to any specific region, and the proportion of disappearances doesn't seem to be any higher here than anywhere else."

She smiled. "No aliens?" she asked.

"I'm not sure," I said. "No evidence of them, certainly, but that doesn't mean they aren't there. After all, Alex, this is pretty much unknown territory for us. We've sent any number of unmanned probes, and a few single scouts and other manned missions, but it's clear from the records that we haven't visited every quadrant within this region, much less every system. And most of our work here, including almost all of the manned expeditions, have been straight mapping missions, not true exploration. Their job is simply to catalog each system for later evaluation, not to investigate any anomalies. Which means that we could have sent a probe into a system with a thriving civilization and not even know it."

"So," she said, touching my hand gently, "was this all a waste of time, then?"

I smiled at her and shook my head. "No," I said. "It had to be looked at. There might have been something there in the records that could have helped us. For that matter, there still might be. It's possible that I'm simply not asking the right questions. Besides," I added, my smile growing slightly, "it let me talk with you. Thanks, Alex. I needed to hear that."

She smiled in return. Leaning forward, she gave me a soft kiss on my cheek. "You're welcome, Tom. That's what friends are for. To tell the truth."

She didn't pull away immediately. For a moment we sat there, staring into each other's eyes, our faces mere inches apart. I wanted to reach up and touch her cheek. I wanted to lean forward and kiss her lips. I wanted to stand up and take her in my arms and just hold her until all the pain and loneliness washed away.

But I didn't do any of that. I couldn't. She was Will's, not mine, and I couldn't bear to be rejected again.

"Thanks," I said again, drawing back slightly and leaning back in my chair. I turned away, then, back to the monitor so that she couldn't see how much it cost me to do that.

Her hand brushed my hair. "Any time, Tom," she said.

A moment later she was gone. I stared at the screen, feeling the emptiness she'd left behind and calling myself all sorts of names. Fool was one of the most common, fool and coward, for that's what I was. A fool for letting myself feel the way that I did, and a coward for not daring to act upon what I felt.

I waited a little while, running a few more passes through the databases and then, after cleaning up our coffee cups, I headed out once more.

Chapter Thirty-Five

We were still thirty-six hours out from our target system when the countdown reached zero. Jamie and I were in our room. Like many of the off-duty personnel on board, we were wracking our brains, trying to come up with an explanation for the two different stretch lines. We were having the same luck as everyone else— explanations were easy to come by, but without more information there was simply no way to know which explanation was correct.

A chime sounded as the countdown went to all zeroes. Jamie and I fell silent, staring at the screen.

Someone was now dead. We could be sure of that. The others could theoretically still be alive—if Lt. Commander Murdoch or one of the others had shut off his oxygen at some point, sacrificing himself in order to preserve his rations for the other two. So it was possible that one or two of our missing crewmen were still alive, but we now had to face the fact that at least one of them was dead.

The timer stopped as soon as it got to zero. It didn't keep going, counting the minutes. There was no point. Maybe if we'd reached the system already, if we thought we might be mere minutes away from finding them, maybe then it would have made sense. This way, though, all it would have been was a cruel reminder of how far off we'd been in our rescue attempt.

The captain must have been thinking along similar lines. Within moments, the stopped timer winked out. In its place, a black stripe appeared, angling across the lower right-hand corner of the display, a visual sign of the loss we all felt.

I couldn't help thinking about the pirates once more, and about that colony ship we'd found, and I couldn't help feeling my guilt once more. Maybe Alex was right and the lieutenant's death wasn't really my fault, but this was— to a degree, anyway. If I'd recognized the trap sooner, we could have sprung their trap sooner, and headed back to Alex that much sooner. I couldn't have shaved thirty-six hours off our response time, but I could have given us something of a head start, if only I'd been quicker.

We kept going, of course. Ours was a mission of mercy, but rescue was only part of our job. There was a mystery to solve, an alien ship to track down, and the bodies, at least, of our missing crewmen to recover. So we kept going, but the mood on board was darker and more depressed than it had been.

Jamie and I kept working on the stretch lines, but it was as hopeless as the rest of our mission. We needed more time to have any hope of saving Murdoch and the others, and we needed more data to have any chance at all of figuring this out.

Six hours later we got what we needed.

"Incoming message," Jamie said, pointing toward the screen.

I nodded. I'd seen the indicator, too.

We both watched, fascinated, as Lt. Wu's latest report scrolled before our eyes.

"It's gone," Jamie said, his voice barely above a whisper. "The alien ship . . . it just vanished."

I nodded again. He was already reaching out, working the controls, calling up the sensor data Lt. Wu had sent along with her report.

"My God," he said. "Would you look at that?"

I was looking, but I could hardly make sense of what I was seeing. Jamie'd had more practice reading these sensor feeds, and as soon as he ran it through his enhanced analysis he laid another line upon the screen. This line, combined with the other two, made a colorful image on the screen, sort of an X with a vertical line through it.

"Look, Tom," he said. "These are the stretch lines we've seen so far. To make things simpler, I've moved them slightly so that they all intersect, even though the ship's two positions were several hundred thousand kilometers apart. Now, this blue line," he pointed to the vertical line, "is the first stretch line we found, and this green one," he moved his finger to indicate the line angling from the top left to the lower right, "is the one we found when the ship reappeared a few days ago."

I nodded. I recognized those lines well enough. I'd been staring at them for hours at a time for these past few days.

"Now this line," he said, pointing to the orange one he'd just added, which stretched from near the top right corner of the screen down toward the lower left corner, "which is only a few degrees off having the same angular separation as the green one, is a new one. Which means that ship just jumped to a new spot."

"Right," I said. "So?"

Jamie grinned at me. "So it gives us a better chance to understand what it's doing. Remember, Tom, each line points in two directions, and we have no way to know which direction is the correct one. That means that with two lines we had four possible combinations, but with only two lines we didn't have a big enough picture to figure it out. Now, with a third line, we have a total of eight different combinations. Let's see if any of them make sense."

Working the controls furiously, he split the screen into eight smaller displays, each one showing the same region of space, and each one centered on the alien vessel's original location. In each separate display, he called up a different combination of the three lines—or, more accurately, he called up a different combination of one half of each line, showing each half as a brightly colored arrow.

Four of the images showed the blue line, representing the first stretch line we'd discovered, pointing straight toward the top of the screen. The other four images showed the blue line starting in the center of the screen and pointing toward the bottom. We knew that the first and third stretch lines, which he'd colored the same blue and green he'd used earlier, were departures, so he only showed those arrows pointing away from the alien ship's original location. The second line was an arrival, so he showed the arrows for that one in orange and pointing toward the spot where we'd first encountered it.

It didn't take him long to do all that. When he'd finished, he paused and looked over at me expectantly.

I studied the screen for several moments, but I couldn't make much sense out of what I was seeing. I mean, I knew what they represented all right, but none of them jumped out at me as being more significant than any of the others.

"I don't get it," I said. "I'm sorry, Jamie, but I just don't see how this helps us."

He nodded and turned back toward the screen. "Look," he said, and I was surprised at the amount of animation in his voice. Normally, for Jamie to get this excited about something, this involved in a puzzle, there had to be a computer involved—or, even better, a new vid game. "You know what these lines represent, right?"

I nodded.

"Good. Then you know we should be able to eliminate half of these right off the bat, right?"

I looked at him. It must have been clear from my expression that I *didn't* know that because he just grinned and said, "We've already made up our minds that the alien ship, when it disappeared that first time, *had* to be travelling in this direction, toward the top of the screen, right? So that means we can eliminate the four images where that line points toward the bottom."

I nodded. Of course, we didn't know that for sure. He was right, we had decided that the alien ship had to have gone in that direction, but we had decided that for our own sake, because it gave us hope for our rescue attempt, and not because there was any real reason for it. Still, it did eliminate half the images, and if none of them turned out to make any sense we could always go back and look at the other four.

Jamie cleared the screen. Splitting it into four equal displays, he once more called up the four images he'd selected as possibles. In all four displays, the three arrows met in the center, with the blue line pointing straight up. In the two top images, the orange arrow started near the top left corner of the display and pointed toward the center; in the two in the bottom row, it started near the lower right corner. Similarly, the two images on the left showed the green arrow pointing toward the upper right corner of the display, and the two in the right hand column showed it pointing down and to the left.

"Two departure vectors," Jamie said, "and one arrival. Four different possible combinations. But which one is it? Which of these four shows us where that ship actually came from, and where it went?"

I looked at the images and then I looked at him. "There's no way to know, Jamie," I said. "Think about it. Not only are these aliens, which means they have a logic all their own, but they have jump technology.

They're not restricted to the same considerations of distance and efficiency that we are."

He started shaking his head before I'd even finished. "You may be right, Tom," he said, that same urgency in his voice, "but we have to assume that you're wrong. After all, like we said earlier, if we can't make some assumptions, then we truly have no hope. Not only will we not be able to figure out which of these four—or even which of the entire eight—is the right one, but we won't know what to do with it even if we did figure it out. Not unless we make some assumptions. And the assumptions that I'm making are that it's one of these four, that these aliens share some sense of logic that we can understand and identify, and that there is an overall pattern to the vectors. Besides, Tom, I'm not sure that I agree that they're not bound by some of the same limitations. I mean, think about it. They can't just wave their hands—or tentacles, or whatever—and make this translation occur. Their process has to require energy, and I'm guessing that, since they're extending their line through space in some fashion, the bigger the jump, the longer their line has to be, and the more energy it takes. I mean, theoretically their line is infinite, but I'm hoping that the length is actually a function of energy. Which means that I think we can count on them making a series of smaller jumps instead of one big one."

I thought about that. "In which case even if we find where they went that first time, it might turn out to merely be a waystation and not their final destination."

He shrugged. "We'll know that in a few more hours. In the meantime, and until I'm forced to give them up, I'm going to operate on these assumptions."

I sighed. "Okay," I said. "You're right." Looking the screen over carefully, I studied each individual image. It didn't take long to figure out which one I'd select. "This one," I said, pointing to the image in the top left corner.

He nodded. "I agree, but why did you pick that one?"

"Process of elimination," I said. "These two on the bottom just don't make sense. Looking at the sequence of the jumps, the alien ship would have first jumped away from the center, toward the top of the screen. Several days later, according to these diagrams, it returned from somewhere out beyond the lower right-hand corner. If what you said is true—or even if we take it as a working assumption—that there are limitations to the distances they travel, then that just doesn't make sense. The distances are simply too great, at least when you compare them to the other possibilities."

He nodded again. "You're right. But why not this one, then?" he asked, pointing to the image at the top right.

"It just doesn't feel right," I said. "I mean, look: this sequence has the ship jumping away to the top, coming back from the top left, and then jumping away again to the lower left. Why? What scenario would make that seem logical?" I shrugged. "I can't come up with one, and so I rejected it."

Jamie looked at me and grinned. "But you *can* come up with a plausible scenario for this other one?"

"Sure," I said. "Look at it. The ship jumps away to the top, comes back from the upper left, and then jumps to the upper right. Just looking at it you get the sense that this ship is patrolling a certain region—and that when something out of the ordinary happened, like when our probe penetrated its hull, it jumped back to the center, back to where its base is." I rubbed at my eyes, feeling suddenly very tired. "We were talking earlier about the possibility of this being a scout ship. This sequence of jumps works very well if that guess was right—a scout ship, or a picket ship, setting the outer lines of defense for a larger force."

"A larger force?" he said. "That would mean that the aliens are still alive."

I nodded. "I know. It makes sense, though. It may not be true, but it makes sense."

Jamie thought that one over. "You're right," he said. "I hadn't come up with that, but you're right. It does make sense." He pointed toward the upper left display. "I'd picked this one, too, but I was thinking more along the lines of there being two ships. I was thinking that the first one might have jumped back toward their base, as you'd suggested, and that a second scout ship then made the next two jumps, coming here from a system somewhere out there to the upper left, checking out the ship we'd left behind, and then jumping out again to another system up and to the right."

I frowned. "I don't buy that one," I said. "If they were checking us out, why would that third jump be to a different system, and not back to the one out beyond the upper left corner? For that matter, why wouldn't they jump back toward the center, like the first ship did? No, Jamie, I think it's the same ship. The only question is, are there more of them out there? And, if so, what are they planning? Exploration? Colonization? Or war?"

He had no answers, of course. None of us did. But several hours later, the *Michelangelo* entered our target system, with battle stations manned and at full defensive posture. Whatever answers lay waiting for us, we were about to find them. Or so we hoped.

Chapter Thirty-Six

Alex and Jamie were on the bridge when we came out of hyperspace. I wanted to be there, too—in fact, I'd have given almost anything to be in the pilot's seat, or even at the Observer station, as we made our slow and careful way into the system. But I couldn't. Instead, I sat hunched before the monitor in my wardroom, picking up sensor feeds and any other information I could.

This system was far enough off the travel lanes to not have a name. According to our charts, it was referred to as GNC18119 and had never been visited by either a manned mission or an unmanned probe. Its star was a red giant, and early spectroscopic analysis indicated that it was old, on the order of three billion years, and on the last legs of its hydrogen store. Sometime within the next few million years, it was likely to go nova.

Five planets swung in orbit around the red sun, all of them in a single plane. The two furthest out were gas giants; the innermost planet, at a distance comparable to Mercury's, was a boiled ball of rock, in a synchronous orbit that always showed the same face to the sun. The other two planets, however, had promise. Massing well within the range of terrestrial worlds, they both lay comfortably within the habitable zone around the red giant. We weren't picking up any signs of life, course—no radio signals, no unexpected radiation, no sign of hyperspace manipulation—but that didn't necessarily mean anything. We hadn't been able to get any readings off that ship, after all, and it was still obviously functional.

Captain Browne had a tough decision to make. On the one hand, this was a totally new situation, and I knew he'd want to proceed cautiously, our defenses on full and our sensors wide open, their data continually analyzed by Jamie's enhanced routine. On the other hand, even though the timer had expired, there was still the hope that one or more of our crewmen would still be alive. Because of that, I knew the captain would want to press forward as quickly as possible.

I didn't know what I would have done in his place, but Captain Browne opted for the slow and cautious route. He took us in carefully, almost hesitantly, with the ship ready to jump to hyperspace at the first sign of trouble. I didn't blame him, not really, but I was on the edge of my seat, glued to my monitor, as we penetrated further into the system.

While I waited for something to happen, I called up the star field that Jamie had used earlier, the one centered on the alien vessel's original location and showing the various stretch lines that corresponded to its possible destinations. Flipping through the various combinations, I settled on the one we had selected as most likely. I'd had a thought, and I wanted to check it out.

Expanding the display, I shifted the focus so that this system we were entering now was at the center. The other location, the place where we'd first encountered the alien ship, was now down near the bottom of the screen. Then, manipulating the controls slightly, I called up a bright yellow circle, centered on this star system and with a radius exactly equal to the length of the blue arrow.

I was playing a hunch. I didn't know what I would learn, even if I was right, but doing something, anything, was better than sitting helplessly on the edge of my seat.

Laying in the green and orange arrows, I extended them to the very edge of the yellow circle. Then, taking a deep breath, I instructed the computer to play a little game. I told it to treat the edge of the circle as a reflective wall, and that first green line as a starting vector. I gave it a little white ball and, launching the ball from the spot where we'd first encountered the alien ship, I sent it out along the green line. I also instructed the computer to leave a white trail behind the ball so that I could follow its progress.

The ball, travelling quite slowly at first, reached the outer edge of the circle and rebounded toward a spot near the top right corner of the screen. When it hit the yellow boundary again it rebounded once more, heading toward the very top of the circle. Within moments it hit the edge for the fifth time and bounded back toward its starting point. As it neared the bottom, I could tell that it was going to miss its first track by a small margin.

Curious, I reached out and sped up the ball. I also instructed the computer to count the number of full circuits it made.

Thirty full circuits later, the white ball met its starting point and began the whole thing over again. On the screen, the white lines made a lacy pattern along the inner edge of the circle.

Sagging back into my chair, I thought about what I had just seen. And the more I thought about it, the more convinced I became that we were right. That alien ship had to be a scout of some sort. Nothing else made sense. The diagram before me showed that, except for the jump it made when we first investigated it, it was on a regular path, just like a border patrol or a defensive picket would be.

This could be good news, I realized. Maybe, just maybe, if there were aliens in the neighborhood, then maybe our missing crewmen were still alive. Surely they would have been discovered almost immediately, and all it would have taken was a little kindness—and a little oxygen—from their captors for them to still be alive.

Quickly I keyed in a short note and sent it, along with my diagrams, to Jamie's terminal on the bridge. I doubted that I was the only one who had spotted this, but I couldn't afford to take any chances. It was important that the captain know about this as soon as possible.

Jamie acknowledged my message and sent one of his own: "Suit up, Tom," he sent. "Suit up and stand by."

I stared at the screen for a moment, unsure what he was talking about. "Suit up" was obvious—but why? I was off the active duty roster.

Shaking my head, I did what he suggested, and then I sat back down to wait.

Chapter Thirty-Seven

The call came two hours later. We were approaching the outer planets, and though our scopes weren't picking up anything unusual yet, Captain Browne was taking no chances. He wanted every available shuttle manned and flying in support of the *Michelangelo*, and that meant that I was temporarily back on active status.

My orders were to select a crew to accompany me and to check out a shuttle as soon as possible.

I would have liked to have Alex and Jamie with me, but that was impossible. Alex was flying her own ship—with Ensign Davies on board as her gunner, no doubt—but Jamie was available. I sent him a quick message and then, scooping up my helmet, I headed toward the hangar bay.

Jamie met me at the ship. "Just me?" he asked, as he looked around. The other two shuttles had already lifted off. I must have been a last-minute decision by the captain—but as long as was letting me fly, I didn't care what reservations he had.

"Just you, buddy," I said. "Just like old times."

Jamie didn't grin, though. "Why?" he asked. "I'm not checked out on the weapons, Tom. You know that.

Why not have some crewmen on board who can help out?"

"You can fire them," I said. "Besides, it won't come to that. At least, it better not. I mean, think about it. These guys have jump technology. They are so far ahead of us that if it comes to a shooting match we won't have a chance."

Which was true, but that wasn't my only reason. The truth was that I didn't want to be responsible for more people than was absolutely necessary. Jamie was my friend. We worked well together. But I didn't want anyone else on board my ship. I didn't want anyone else's deaths on my conscience.

"Come on, buddy," I said. "Let's go."

It wasn't like old times, though. Jamie and I had flown uncounted hours together back on Brighthome, once I'd earned my flames. Assuming I wasn't grounded for daydreaming in class, we'd take our old, reconditioned runabout up each Saturday, milking every minute of our six hours of freedom—or at least as much freedom as we could find in a place like that.

But that had been play. It had been adventure, and excitement, and exploration. It had been *fun*. This was none of that. This was real.

Alex had the center position. Lt. Freeman was on her left, Jamie and I were on her right. Once we'd formed up with them, the three of us moved out ahead of the *Michelangelo*. Our job was to extend the *Michelangelo*'s sensor range.

The two gas giants were unremarkable. We could detect no sign of life on either planet, and no indication that anyone had ever been there at all. Of course, there could have been an entire civilization on both those worlds at one point, and with the intense gravity and atmospheric pressure all signs would have been eradicated shortly after the civilizations collapsed.

The third planet was my pick as the likeliest candidate. It was slightly larger than the other world whose orbit lay within the temperate zone, and it just seemed more likely to have supported life at some point. But there was nothing there now.

We gave this one a closer look than we'd given the gas giants, searching for signs of anything from a world-spanning civilization to the smallest outpost. We found nothing. No signs that there had ever been free-flowing water on the surface. No signs of settlements, large or small. Nothing.

Nearing the second planet, however, our boards lit up with a series of unexplained readings.

"We've got something, Tom," Jamie said.

A sudden sense of relief washed over me, mixed in with no small amount of fear. We'd pinned an awful lot of hope on our decision to come in this direction, and we'd gotten lucky.

"Great," I said. "What've we got?"

Jamie's hands flew over his board, refining his readings. After a moment, however, he sat back and looked over at me. "I don't know," he said. "I've never seen anything like this."

My radio chatter confirmed his report. The other two shuttles were picking up the same readings, but no one— including the technicians back on the *Michelangelo*— could make sense of them.

"Details," I snapped. "Tell me what you've got."

Jamie turned back toward his board. "Anomalies, Tom. I'm picking up several dozen anomalous readings in apparent orbit around the second planet. They seem to be spherical objects, ranging from approximately two meters in diameter to just over ten meters, but my readings don't make any sense. Hyperwave detection shows mass off the scale. Spectroscopic analysis is negative. Scanner readings are negative. No detectable EMF around any of the objects. Radiation output is zero.

Reflectivity is nearly one hundred percent." He looked over at me again. "I can go on, Tom, but these readings just don't add up."

"What do you mean the scanner readings are negative? We can see them, right? And they register on the hyperwave grid. So the scanners *have* to be able to pick them up."

Jamie just stared at me. "I know, Tom," he said. "But they can't. It's like those things aren't really there, like the scanners are just slipping past them." He sighed. "I don't know, Tom. I can't explain it."

We were drawing closer now, close enough that I could call up a visual.

The planet we were approaching was dead. There was no other way to describe it. Mostly grey and white, the surface was heavily cratered, and showed the smooth flow plains of ancient, intense volcanic activity as well. There wasn't much of an atmosphere, just a thin layer of heavy gases. Early speculation among the science staff was that there had been some major cataclysm here at some point in the past. Perhaps a series of comets had hit the planet, or perhaps it had been the site of a terrible war. Either way, something had cracked the mantle in several places, essentially repaving the entire surface of the planet.

That event, or series of events, had also boiled away most of the atmosphere, leaving the planet unprotected from asteroids and meteor showers. The scientists couldn't say for sure if there had ever been a civilization there or not.

That was interesting, and worth speculating about, but the planet itself wasn't the most interesting find. Instead, we were all more curious about the objects in orbit around it.

There were dozens of them, and except for their size they all looked exactly alike: shiny, silvery balls hanging high above the dead planet. There was something else, though, something undefinable, yet definitely there. I had the feeling as I looked at them that there was something else there, something I wasn't seeing. It was as though my gaze was sliding past something—something important, something I just couldn't quite see.

"It's like they're not really there," I said, my voice little more than a whisper, "as if they were holes opening up into a place we're not equipped to see."

Jamie looked at me, then down at his board, and then back at me. "No," he said, shaking his head. "They're there, all right. They're real. The mass detector confirms that."

"So what are they?" I asked. "And why are they here? I mean, what makes this planet special?"

He couldn't answer that, of course. No one could. Not yet.

Settling back into our seats, we started a series of scanner runs that, with a little luck, would give us some answers.

Chapter Thirty-Eight

The ships came out of nowhere.

Captain Browne had sent Lt. Freeman to check out the innermost planet. No one expected to find anything of interest there, but the captain was a thorough man and he wanted all the possibilities covered.

Lt. Freeman had reported back, saying there was nothing there—no signs of life, no unusual readings, and no silvery balls—and started on his way back. That was when we picked up our first sign of trouble.

"Captain," that was Lt. Freeman's voice, coming in over an open channel, "I'm picking up several objects headed your way—visuals only, sir; scanners aren't showing anything. Bearing two four three and one six eight. They're almost on top of you, sir."

I looked over at Jamie, automatically mapping those bearings in my head. "The gas giants," I said.

"But we checked there," Jamie said, his hands flying over his controls. "There was nothing there."

"I know. These must have come from somewhere else. They must be using the mass of the planets to hide their approach. It's the only way they could sneak up on us."

"Got 'em," Jamie said. "I show eight ships, four in each

204

group, range approximately four hundred thousand kilometers and closing fast."

"Configurations?" I asked.

"I can't tell," he said. "I'm picking them up on hyperwave, but not on any of the other sensors. From their mass readings, though, I'd say six are the size of scout ships and two are cruiser equivalents."

"Pirates," I said, thinking about the one that got away from us earlier. Their stealth technology was the only thing I knew of that could explain that.

Jamie nodded. "It's got to be."

New orders were coming in then. Breaking orbit, Alex and I spread out, moving to positions on either side of the *Michelangelo*.

Jamie looked over at me, once, and I knew what he was thinking. And he was right. I should have selected a larger crew.

"It's up to you, buddy," I said. "You've got the guns."

He nodded. Putting his scanners on automatic, he slid over to weapons control and brought his board to life.

We didn't have time for him to get comfortable. My own board showed him powering up the various weapon systems and running them through a short check list. Then the pirates were within range and we were out of time.

My guess was that if we hadn't spotted them the pirates would have simply continued on in a straight line, attacking the *Michelangelo* as each one came within range. As soon as we took up our new positions, however, it became clear to them that they had lost the element of surprise—though just barely—and so they formed up into two distinct attack groups, close enough to support each other, but far enough apart that we had to pick our targets with care.

My hands were sweaty inside my gloves. I wasn't ready for this. I could fly the ship, and I could follow orders, but I hadn't had any training on battle tactics or techniques.

"Easy, Tom," Alex said, her voice coming to me on a private channel. "Just stay relaxed."

"No problem," I said, but even I could hear the nervousness in my voice.

"Just stay focussed," she said. "There are more of them, but we've got better guns, better armor, and better ships. All you need to do is to maintain position and let your gunner do the rest."

"Jamie's my gunner," I said.

She was silent for a moment. "Who else is on board your shuttle?"

"No one," I said. "It's just the two of us. I didn't think—"

"Never mind," she said. "It'll be fine. Trust your armor. Let them get close enough to make the shots easy, and tell Jamie to use his blasters, not his missiles. We're having trouble acquiring any sort of decent scanner lock on their stealth ships, and we don't need a bunch of missiles flying around looking for targets."

"Understood," I said.

"And, Tom?"

"Yes?"

"Stay relaxed."

"Sure," I said. "No problem," but the tension was still there in my voice.

"Remember the *Hobo One*? This is just like that."

That was the name we'd given the runabout we'd used back on Brighthome. I nodded, and for a moment I actually missed the relative peace and quiet of Brighthome. Then the moment passed, and I had to focus on my job once more.

The first pirate ships broke ranks, then, starting their attack run.

"Good luck," Alex said. She was gone, off the radio before I could reply.

The other ships were moving now, too, forming up into pairs and powering toward us in waves.

"Tom?" Jamie called, his voice every bit as scared sounding as my own. "What do I do, Tom?"

I had no idea. But I couldn't tell him that. I was the pilot. I was in charge. And he was looking to me for guidance. That fact that I didn't feel qualified to give any guidance simply didn't make any difference.

Taking a deep breath, I said, "Just pick a target, buddy," I said. "Stick with your blasters for now. Pick a target, let it come as close as you can, and then fire. Stay with it, and stay focussed."

"Okay," he said, but his voice was still shaky.

"You can do it," I said.

He didn't answer me, but my board showed that he had targeted one of the ships in the first wave on our side. I nodded and turned my attention back to my own responsibilities.

These pirates were good, I had to say that for them. Better than I had expected, even. As I watched them flying in their tight formations I realized that they must have called in their best pilots and given them their best ships. I didn't know if that meant they had already discovered this place and were trying to keep it a secret, or if they just wanted to take out a Space Guard ship that badly.

Alex and I had taken up positions slightly ahead and to each side of the *Michelangelo*. Given the bearings the pirate ships were on, that meant that they had to fly across our bows to get at the *Michelangelo*. Our job was to slow them down, not to draw their fire, and I was prepared to retreat at any moment, to pull back within the protection of the bigger guns on board the *Michelangelo*.

The first wave was a fake, and Jamie had fallen for it. They came in straight at us, as though daring us to fire, but then veered off suddenly, the one Jamie was tracking going left, away from the *Michelangelo*, the other going right, toward our mother ship. Jamie hesitated for a moment, then switched targets. As he did so, though, that ship veered again, pulling back. Behind it, the second wave came in, heading straight toward us.

Jamie cried out, in anger and frustration, and switched targets once again, but by then the second wave of ships was in range and firing their blasters.

I hesitated a moment, waiting to see which ship Jamie was aiming at, and then turned the nose of the ship slightly, pointing her nose directly at the other pirate vessel. I wanted to give it the smallest target possible. In doing so, I increased the target for the other pirate ship, but I was trusting that Jamie would take that out before it could do too much damage.

Trust your armor, Alex had said. And she was right. The pirates had about three seconds of concentrated fire, but we survived it, though the attack stripped away most of our forward shielding. Then Jamie's blasters found their mark and one of the enemy ships exploded. I heard him gasp, and whisper something that might have been either a prayer or an apology, and then the *Michelangelo* opened fire behind us, her main batteries discharging, and the second pirate vessel followed the first.

I had time for a quick glance to see how Alex was faring. She and her crew apparently had not fallen for the pirate trick, and had taken out both ships in the second wave. Even as I watched, she was bringing her ship to a new position, making sure that neither of the first two could get past her. As far as I could tell, her ship had not yet been touched.

I smiled, but only for a moment. We had taken out the second wave, too, with a little help from the guns on board the *Michelangelo*, but I had lost track of the first wave.

I glanced over at the scanners, but they were no help. They couldn't detect the stealth ships.

"There!" Jamie cried, pointing toward the ship that had veered toward the *Michelangelo*. It was being painted by the big ship's main blasters, and showed up clearly against the field of stars. A moment later the pirate vessel exploded.

But where was the last one?

"Bogey on your tail, Tom." That was Alex, and for the first time I heard the tension in her voice. "Accelerate to oh-five-oh degrees, now."

I didn't stop to think. I simply did what she'd said, bringing the shuttle to a new heading and hitting the jets. My board lit up suddenly, and I knew we were taking a full blaster shot in our rear section.

"I'm on him," Alex said. "Closing fast. Hang in there, Tom."

I veered left, then lifted the nose and came back right, trying to shake the ship behind us. The blaster beam fell away, but found us again as I straightened out of that last maneuver.

"Almost there, Tom. Almost . . ."

The lights on my board winked out as my rear display showed yet another pirate ship destroyed. Jamie let out a whoop, but I had a sudden sinking feeling. That was six ships, I realized, which left two, both of them cruisers and both of them on Alex's side of the *Michelangelo*— but she wasn't over there any more. She had come over here to help me out.

"Look sharp," I said to Jamie. "I want to know where those last two ships are."

Blaster fire fell upon the *Michelangelo*, and we could see one of the pirate ships off her starboard bow, firing from close range. Immediately, the *Michelangelo* went into a roll, preventing the blaster fire from falling on any single spot of shielding for long.

I nodded to myself. They wouldn't be able to return fire effectively that way, but at least it would buy time for help to arrive.

That hope died, however, when, beside me, an indicator on Jamie's scanner board lit up.

"Ship killers away," I said, trying to keep my voice calm. "Looks like the pirate launched two missiles, both at the *Michelangelo*."

"I'm on it," Jamie said.

I brought our ship around, heading toward an intercept with those missiles. This was a dangerous move. With our forward shielding nearly gone, I was presenting our weakest area toward the enemy, but I had no choice. We couldn't let those missiles through.

I glanced at my rear display, checking on Alex's position, and my hands froze on my controls. Alex had come around, changing course to follow me in, but that wasn't what had stopped me.

I had just found the last pirate ship. It was on her tail, and closing fast. Coming in directly behind her drive section, it was in the one place her own guns couldn't reach.

For a moment I couldn't breathe, couldn't think, couldn't act. Alex had come to my rescue, and in so doing had put herself and the *Michelangelo* in terrible danger.

"Alex!" I cried. "Behind you!"

I started to turn the ship, to return the help she had given us, but her voice cut me off. "I see it, Tom," she said. All the nervousness and tension were gone from her voice. "Stay on course."

"But—"

"No buts. Protect the *Michelangelo* at all costs."

"But—"

"Stay on course, Tom. Dammit, do as I say."

Behind her, the pirate ship opened fire, its blasters falling full upon her rear shielding. I saw her juke, trying to shake the beam, trying to come around in order to return fire, but the pilot stayed with her every move. Before us, the *Michelangelo* had come out of her roll and had begun to return fire. She had taken out the missiles, but there were four more heading her way, and the concentrated blaster fire was starting to take its toll.

"I'm sorry, Alex," I said and turned back toward the *Michelangelo*.

Moments later, Jamie opened fire. His first shots missed, passing in front of the oncoming missiles, but as soon as his blasters opened up the *Michelangelo* shifted targets from the missiles to the ship that was firing them.

Jamie held his guns steady, allowing the missiles to fly right into the barrage he was laying down. In less than five seconds, all four missiles and the ship that had launched them were gone.

Quickly, I turned back toward Alex, but it was too late. She had veered away from the *Michelangelo*, and away from us, making sure that the pirate behind her would not be able to continue its attack on us when it had finished with her. That had taken her out of the range of our guns, and there was nothing that we could do.

I could see that her rear shielding was gone. She had managed to roll slightly, bringing the blaster fire onto her lateral shielding, but even that was almost gone. She had tried every trick, and I was proud of her for what she had done, but she was out of things to do.

Tears stung my eyes, and I almost missed what happened next.

A third ship flashed onto my screens, guns blazing, flying out of the sun and directly toward the last remaining pirate ship. I let out a yell, thrusting my hands into the air, as I recognized the new ship. It was Lt. Freeman. He had used the pirates' own trick against them, counting on the sun's gravity well to disguise his approach.

The pirate ship tried to turn, tried to launch a couple of ship killers, but it never had a chance. Lt. Freeman's guns found it, and it was gone, its missiles exploding before they had even cleared the launch tubes.

It was over. We had won. Eight pirate ships, all of them stealth capable, and yet we had won.

Jamie racked his guns and came back to his scanner station. When I looked over at him, through the clear faceplate on his helmet, I saw sweat pouring down his face, but what took my breath away and stilled the moment of joy growing within my heart were the tears I saw in his eyes.

We had won, I knew, but at what price?

I reached out and touched his arm, but I didn't say anything.

A minute later, Alex's voice came over my radio. "Nice job, everyone," she said. "Now let's go home."

Still without saying a word, I brought the shuttle around and headed back toward the *Michelangelo*.

Chapter Thirty-Nine

Pouring out of our shuttles, we all met once more in the hangar bay, Lt. Freeman and his crew, Alex and her crew, and Jamie, recovered now, and I, grinning, yelling, and pounding each other on the back. We were all still wearing our space suits, but had our helmets thrown back. All of us were sweaty and disheveled, but none of us cared. We were alive, and we were safe, and we were home.

The best moment for me was when I watched Alex come out of her ship, wisps of smoke still lifting off the aft section. Behind her, the six crewmen she'd taken with her waited to debark. The thing was, Ensign Davies wasn't among them. Her gunner was Johnson, who had manned the guns for me during that fateful boarding run on the derelict.

The fact that Will Davies wasn't there might have been a bad sign, I knew. It could have meant that Alex cared for him too much to take him into danger. Except that none of us had expected a battle.

No, I preferred to think that there might be some hope for me after all.

Lt. Freeman, Alex, and I had a brief moment

together before our duties called us away from the
hangar bay. We stood there, the three of us, a small
space of silence in a room filled with noise, and we
merely looked at each other. There were no words to
describe how we felt, no amount of thanks any of us
could give to the others.

Alex moved first, stepping forward to give each of us
a hug, Lt. Freeman first, then me.

Holding her like that, a wave of intense emotion
washed over me and my arms tightened around her.
What I felt was a crazy mixture of longing and hope and
sadness and frustration and probably half a dozen other
less readily identifiable emotions.

"Alex," I murmured, reaching up to touch her hair.
"I'm so sorry—"

But she didn't let me finish. "Shh, Tom," she said,
pulling her head back so that she could look at me. "It's
all right. I understand."

"But—" I started. Again she cut me off.

"Later," she said. "We'll talk later." And then she gave
me a quick, sweet kiss, so brief that few people in the
hangar bay would have even noticed, and yet long enough
that I could feel the touch of her lips tingling on mine
for moments afterward.

As she pulled away, the lieutenant smiled at me,
rested his hand briefly on my shoulder, and shook my
hand. "Good work out there, Mr. Jenkins," he said, and
then turned away. It wasn't much, but it was enough.

The little impromptu celebration broke up then.
There were hours of debriefing ahead of us before we
could truly let ourselves celebrate. I watched Alex walk
out of the hangar bay, her head high and a spring in
her step, and I knew in that moment that what I had
told myself earlier—that I had given up my hopes of
a future with her—was a lie. It was a hopeless dream,
but a powerful one, and one that I would never be able
to let go.

Jamie clapped me on the back, pulling me out of my thoughts.

"Hey, hero," I said, smiling at him. "You ready?"

He nodded. "Let's go."

Chapter Forty

The next few hours were the most hectic I'd spent on board the *Michelangelo*—even more than that first week, when Jamie and I were tying to learn our jobs, trying to make a place for ourselves, trying to memorize the layout of the ship, and just plain trying to adjust. There were debriefing sessions, with different officers grilling us both individually and in groups. Mostly, though, there was work, examining the scanner logs, probing the planet, studying those silvery balls, looking for anything that might be a clue to the fate of Murdoch and the other missing crewmen.

That night, after dinner, we were being grilled once more. Alex was there, and Johnson, her gunner. Jamie was there, too, and I was the fourth. Lt. Freeman had missed much of the battle and was not present.

This was another one of our interminable debriefing sessions, answering yet another round of questions about the battle, about the tactics the pirates had used, and about our impressions of their new stealth capabilities. The officer grilling us, Lt. Commander Laura Dreyfuss, who served as commanding officer during the third shift, was showing us recorded images of the various fights and asking questions about each particular movement. The images were computer constructs, reenactments of the actual scenes pieced together from the scanner logs of all four ships.

Jamie, sitting on my right, was paying more attention to the video than to her questions. That was all right, though. He'd been at the weapons console for most of it and had been too focussed on his targets to comment on the battle as a whole. Johnson, sitting at my far left, on the other side of Alex, was also not paying a lot of attention. Most of the questions so far had been aimed at Alex and myself.

We were discussing the pirate ship that ended up on our tail. Lt. Commander Dreyfuss was pointing at the screen, asking me how I'd let the enemy ship into such a tactically superior position, when Jamie sat up straight and pointed at the screen.

"Hey," he said. "Did you see that?"

On screen, our little shuttle was taking a beating. The pirate was firing on us, and had just retargeted us after my evasive maneuvers.

"Replay that last sequence," he said.

The lieutenant commander gave Jamie a sharp look, but then indicated that he should take the controls. He did so, and the five of us watched as he ran the images back a few seconds.

"Watch," he said. "Watch their blasters when Tom veers right."

I remembered that moment all too well, my board flashing at me, indicating the damage we'd already taken from their fire. Their beam had slipped off to my left as I dodged. I had assumed that they had ceased firing until they could lock onto me again, but watching the images scroll past I could see that I was wrong. They'd kept their blaster fire on maximum as they attempted to reacquire my ship.

"There," Jamie said. "That was it."

We all saw it that time. Even Johnson sat up straighter in his chair, leaning forward slightly to get a better view.

In adjusting their aim, hunting us with their blasters, their fire had fallen briefly on one of the silvery balls in orbit around the second planet.

"Let's see that again," Alex said.

Lt. Commander Dreyfuss reached out and took the controls back from Jamie. Orienting the view on the ball, she set the images to cycle over a two-second period, starting right before the blaster fire fell upon it and ending shortly after it stopped. At the bottom of the screen, she called up additional scanner information on the ball—energy output, spectroscopic analysis, mass readings, diameter, and other, similar data.

The mass readings were off the scale, and did not change with the blaster fire. The other readings—all but one—were negative, and also did not change. The one reading that did change was the diameter; it increased very slightly, as though it was absorbing the energy of the pirates' blaster beam. When the beam fell away, seeking out my shuttle once more, the silvery ball maintained its new size.

"What do you think that means?" Jamie asked.

I didn't know which of us he was asking, but none of us had an answer for him.

Lt. Commander Dreyfuss left us then, taking this new development to the captain. The rest of us stayed behind, talking things over and trying to come up with some sort of explanation. Between the four of us, we thought up all sorts of ideas and possibilities—some of them pretty wild—but none of them held up for very long. Then Alex reached out for the controls.

Working quickly, she did some fairly basic math and calculated how much energy had fallen on that silvery ball from the blasters, and how much size it had gained. Then, taking the smallest ball in orbit as a starting point, she calculated how much light from the red giant would have had to fall for one of them to grow to the size of the largest one in orbit.

Dazed, she sat back in his chair, an impossibly large number on the screen. If both her calculations and Jamie's assumptions were correct, and that large ball had started out the same size as the smallest one, then it had been in orbit around the second planet for slightly more than sixteen million years.

"That can't be right," I said.

"I know," she said. "But it was worth trying." Reaching out, she cleared away her calculations, and we went back to discussing alternatives.

"There's only one thing I can think of to explain all these different readings," Jamie said an hour later. We had been silent for the past five minutes, out of ideas and staring at the screen in silent frustration. "I hesitate to even bring it up, though," he said. "It's really a pretty silly idea."

Alex reached out and touched his hand. "What is it?" she asked.

Jamie looked over at me. "I was thinking about pocket universes," he said. "I know it's stupid, but—"

"No, wait," Alex said. "Go on, Jamie. Please."

He glanced over at me again, and I got the distinct impression that there was something he didn't want me to say or do. I just didn't have any idea what.

"Well," he said, "I've been doing a bit of work in this area, and it seems to me that some of these readings may be consistent with the interface between our universe and another one." He blushed then, only slightly, but on Jamie even a slight blush showed up easily.

Johnson let out a sound that was somewhere between a snort and a cough. "You mean that's why the mass readings are so high?" he asked. "Because each of those contains an entire universe?"

Alex glared at him, but Jamie simply shook his head. "Not at all. Remember that our mass readings are not really mass readings at all. I mean, we don't exactly go out there and push on an object to measure its resistance and determine its mass. Instead, we use a variant of the hyperwave detection grid, which looks at the warping of the space-time fabric. The more it's warped, the more mass we assume an object has. But, in this case, we may be wrong. If I'm right, and these are pocket universes, they would warp the fabric of our universe in the same way as an incredibly massive object."

"Oh," Johnson said.

"You know," I said, "that's not a bad idea. Our notion of their jump technology is based on the idea that they can work with the fabric of our universe—that they can, in effect, translate from our three-dimensional universe into another, single dimensional one, and use that to travel. If they can do that, then they obviously know a lot more than we do about other dimensions and other universes. If such a thing is possible, I have no trouble believing that these people, whoever they were, would have learned how."

Alex nodded. "I like it," she said. "I don't understand it, but I like it."

Jamie reached for the computer controls. "If I'm right," he said, "we should be able to duplicate this, or at least come relatively close."

He worked the keys quickly, too fast for me to follow. I could tell that he was calling up some files from somewhere, but I couldn't tell what they were or where they were coming from.

"Here," he said. "Look. These are mathematical models of different universes, places where one or more of the defining factors is slightly different from ours. In this one, for example," he pointed to a group of equations, "the value of G, the force of gravity, is higher than in ours. In this one the nuclear force is weaker. You can play with these values all day, creating some of the most bizarre environments imaginable."

"Okay," Johnson said, ignoring the look Alex was giving him. "Say you're right. Say these *are* pocket universes. Why? What good are they? And why would a race with this sort of incredible technology leave them in orbit around their planet?"

"They're not in orbit," Jamie said. "Not really. If I'm right, they're not really *here* at all. What we're seeing are interfaces, not physical objects, and so they can't really be in orbit. I think they're tied to the planet in some way, but at a much more fundamental level than simple gravity and inertia. Otherwise, some of the orbits would have decayed over time, and I don't think that has happened."

"All right," Johnson said, "but that still doesn't answer my question. What good are they?"

"Escape," Alex said. "Think about it, Johnson. We've already seen that this planet was the site of some tremendous cataclysmic events. Perhaps they created these pocket universes to escape whatever it was."

But Jamie was shaking his head. "I don't think so," he said. "Remember, they have jump technology. They could escape to other areas of this universe just as easily, if not more easily, than creating these pocket universes."

Alex nodded, a thoughtful expression on her face. "Then why?" she asked, echoing Johnson's question.

Jamie frowned and looked over at me. I shrugged. This was all new to me. He'd obviously been thinking about it for some time, and had figured parts of it out, but he hadn't shared it with me.

"I think it was war," he said. "It's the only explanation I can come up with that makes any sort of sense at all."

"What do you mean?" Johnson asked, but I noticed that the sarcastic edge was gone from his voice.

"I think they were at war with another race, perhaps one that also had jump technology. Or it could have been an offshoot of its own race, I suppose, some sort of rival colony or country, but given their obvious advancement

I prefer to think that it was another race entirely. If so, and if their enemies did have jump technology, then there would have been no escape for them anywhere in our universe."

He paused to let that sink in. Then he went on, "But I still don't think they created these universes to escape into. Like I was saying earlier, these aren't really alternate worlds. It's not like they could simply create a universe where their enemies didn't exist. Instead, they're entirely new universes, ones where the physical laws, even the physical constants, are different—and there just aren't that many combinations that can sustain life. So I don't think they created them to escape into. I think they created them to survive."

Alex, Johnson, and I all exchanged a puzzled glance.

Jamie saw that and grinned sheepishly. "I'm not trying to be vague," he said. "I'm just trying to explain something that I don't fully understand myself. You see, my best guess, based mostly on the behavior of that ship that led us here, is that these pocket universes have only one key value different from ours. If I'm right—and I may very well not be—they've altered the arrow of time."

Alex frowned. "Why?" she asked.

"You mean they've made time run backwards?" I asked at the same moment.

Jamie shook his head. "I don't think they've made time run backwards," he said. "And I don't think they've merely slowed it down. I think they've stopped time entirely. I think these little pocket universes are the most practical demonstration of a stasis field I've ever seen— and, what's more, they don't require any power. Once they're created, they exist forever, or until the same technology that created them reverses the process."

There was a stunned silence as the three of us took that in. I expected Johnson to say something cutting again, but he seemed to be the first to grasp the implications of what Jamie was saying.

"And that ship . . ." he said, his voice soft and full of wonder.

" . . . was not a scout ship at all," Jamie said. "It was an ambulance, patrolling a certain sector of their battle zone, finding casualties and bringing them back here, in stasis so that the wounded would survive until they could be treated."

"Whoa," I said. "I'm trying to stay with you here, Jamie, but you lost me there."

He nodded. "Look, this is all just speculation, right? But if we're going to figure this out, we have to come up with an explanation that fits all the facts. Take that planet down there. It's been blasted back to a primordial ball. Is it possible that what happened down there was simply some type of natural disaster, a planet-wide catastrophe of a magnitude we've never seen before? Sure, it's possible, but that doesn't fit with the other facts—namely that alien vessel that led us here. I mean, if it was a natural disaster, how can we explain that ship, and the pattern of its jumps?"

He looked around the room at the three of us. "No," he said, "the only thing I've been able to come up with to explain *all* the facts is if this race, whoever they were, was at war. The destruction of the planet was done as an act of war, either by their enemies or by themselves, perhaps a mass suicide as a gesture of defiance, or to avoid capture, or to keep vital secrets or technology from falling into their enemy's hands.

"And that explains the ship . . . but not as a scout ship, or even part of a picket line of defense. Remember that it didn't react to our presence at all. It allowed Alex's shuttle to come within ten meters of it, and Lt. Commander Murdoch and his party were able to make physical contact with its hull, all without it ever reacting. Does that sound like a defensive ship? I mean, if we'd been the enemy, we could have destroyed it with limpet mines or other devices."

Jamie looked around the room again, but none of us was ready to interrupt him. "That ship didn't react until we entered one of its hatches," he said. "Think about it. We'd approached it without giving off any kind of recognized signals. That could mean we were an enemy vessel, but it could also mean that we were one of the good guys, badly damaged in battle and unable to send any kind of friend-or-foe identification. So how would a ship like that, functioning like one of those old medivac helicopters that airlifted wounded soldiers from battle, react to an unannounced presence like ours? If we were good guys, it would want to wrap the injured people in stasis, in one of these pocket universes, and take them back for medical help. Which," he added, "is exactly what it did."

I was stunned by what he was saying, but I could see both Alex and Johnson nodding in sudden understanding.

"And," Johnson said, "if we were the enemy—"

Alex cut him off. "It would want to do the same thing: wrap us in stasis and take us back to where we could be imprisoned and questioned."

Jamie nodded. "Exactly. That ship has to be an ambulance of some sort, but with one hell of a security program built into it."

"And it's still functioning after all this time," Johnson said. "My God, think about what that means. This race had jump technology, pocket universes, and the ability to build ships that would last for millions of years, and yet they were obviously in a terrible, terrible war. Makes you wonder what their enemy was like, doesn't it?"

We all nodded at that. The universe was a vast and mostly empty place, and we had explored only a tiny fraction of it. If something like this was lying hidden in our own backyards, what would we find when we got out further among the stars?

That was an exciting thought, but a scary one, too.

"All right," Johnson said. "That ship was an ambulance,

designed to pick up injured soldiers, ones whose ships
were no longer capable of making it back to base. It
would encapsulate them in their own pocket universe,
one where time simply didn't pass, and then it would
take them back here for treatment. Only something went
wrong. Someone—or something—destroyed all life on
this planet. But this ship, apparently unmanned and
following a preprogrammed set of instructions, has spent
all this time jumping from place to place, doing its job
and looking for survivors. Wow."

Alex came to her feet, almost leaping out of her chair,
and started pacing. "Wait a minute," she said. "If what
you're saying is true, then that means that there are aliens
inside those bubbles—living aliens, I mean, not just
artifacts and bodies."

Jamie nodded. "They'd be sixteen million years old,
but for them not a single moment of time has passed
since their pocket universes were formed. The moment
their pocket universes are dissolved they will be right
back in our universe, in the exact same condition as when
they went in."

Alex paused to look at him. Suddenly, a huge grin
burst across her face and she started pacing excitedly
again. "Jamie," she said, "if you're right, then that means
that Mr. Murdoch and the others—"

"—are alive and well," Jamie said. "If I'm right. The
problem is, we won't know for a very long time."

Alex stopped as suddenly as if he'd slapped her.
"What?" she said. "Why?"

"We don't have the technology," Jamie said. "We can't
even look inside those bubble universes, much less figure
out how to reverse the process. But we will. Now that
we know about it, we can start studying them, learning
how they work, learning how to create them and how
to undo them. And we have that ship, too, which has
the capability to turn these things on and off. All we have
to do is figure out how."

It wasn't going to be as simple as that, I knew, especially since we couldn't even enter that ship without triggering its automatic programming. But that didn't take away from the fact that Jamie had just given us something we hadn't had since the countdown had reached zero: he had given us hope.

"Come on," Alex said. "Let's go report this to someone."

On the way out, I pulled Jamie aside for a moment.

"Hey," I said to him, softly enough that Alex and Johnson couldn't hear. "Pocket universes? When were you ever 'doing a bit of work in this area'?"

He grinned and blushed again, looking down at his feet. "I was hoping you weren't going to bring that up. It was a vid game I was playing back before we left Brighthome, a strategy game where you had to design universes for different types of beings. It was more complicated than that, I mean there were fights and chases and stuff, but that was the main idea. Anyway, I thought of it the other day, when we first saw the readings from those silver balls, and I just couldn't get it out of my head." He looked up at me suddenly. "You won't tell anyone, will you?" he asked.

I laughed. I couldn't help it. Reaching out, I punched him lightly on the shoulder. "Your secret's safe with me, buddy," I said.

Turning, then, we hurried to catch up with Alex and Johnson.

Chapter Forty-One

It turned out that Jamie was right—or at least that other people agreed with him. The irony was that he didn't get any of the credit for discovering it.

When Alex, as the highest ranking member among us, made her report, she found out that we weren't the only ones to think of this. Several different teams, in fact, had come up with a number of Jamie's ideas already. We would have known this if our investigations had been part of our official assignments, but since we were merely talking on our own time, no one had shared their findings with us.

Jamie took it well, though. He didn't get his name in any of the reports, and didn't receive any official recognition, but the captain and all the other officers were aware of what he had done. If he'd had any worries about his ability to fit in, or his qualification to wear the blue jumpsuit of the Space Guard, those fears had been answered.

Mine, however, had not.

Now that things had calmed down a bit, and Lt. Commander Dreyfuss had been officially reassigned as executive officer of the *Michelangelo*, Captain Browne was able to call his review board to examine my actions in the events that led to the death of Lt. Ramirez. I waited alone in the library, nervous and pacing, while they reviewed the scanner and communication logs.

It was Alex who brought me the news. She came into the library, a solemn expression on her face, and a very official-looking sealed document in her hand. Without a word, she marched up to me, saluted, and held the document out to me.

"What's this?" I asked, my voice thin and high.

"The results of the board," she said, still standing at attention. "I requested permission to deliver it."

"What's it say?"

But she shook her head. "It's an official communication," she said. "You'll have to read it for yourself." Then she winked at me.

I took the envelope with shaking hands. I remembered what she had said to me earlier, about how Lt. Ramirez's death wasn't my fault, and I wanted her to be right. A part of me believed her already, maybe a large part, and that part very much wanted to be able to continue to wear the Space Guard blues. But another part of me refused to let go of my blame and guilt, and that part of me knew what this message said.

Slowly, I tore the end off the envelope and pulled out a piece of paper. Holding my breath, I unfolded it and read the report.

It didn't take long. The findings were short and simple.

"This board hereby finds Honorary Apprentice Guardsman Thomas Jenkins blameless in the death of Lt. Enrigo Ramirez. It is the finding of this board that Apprentice Jenkins showed initiative and that his actions were reasonable and in keeping with the finest traditions of the Guard. No disciplinary action is called for, and this board hereby reinstates Apprentice Jenkins to full active duty effective immediately."

That was it.

I looked up from the paper, the beginnings of a smile on my face, and Alex stepped forward. "I told you," she said, kissing me lightly on the cheek.

I couldn't believe it. "Thanks," I said. "For everything."

"You're welcome, Tom," she said. Then, her voice growing suddenly serious, she added, "But there's something else."

"Yes?" I said. I didn't like that new tone in her voice. Her sudden seriousness was out of place with the news she'd just brought me, and I found myself sobering as well.

"I heard you've been checking into that colony ship we discovered."

I nodded, but I found myself wondering how she'd found out about that. No one—not even Jamie—knew that I'd been doing that. "That's true," I said. "Research like that isn't off limits or anything, is it?"

She shook her head. "No, Tom. Nothing like that. But I'm guessing that you didn't find what you were looking for. Am I right?"

I paused, unsure how to answer that. This was a highly personal matter, after all, and certainly not Space Guard business. On the other hand, Alex was a friend, and I fervently hoped that one day she would be much more than a friend.

I nodded again, though more slowly than the last time. "You're right," I said. "If you know what I was doing, you probably also know what I was looking for. Well, I didn't find it."

"I did."

That rocked me. My head jerked back sharply as though I'd just been slapped. "You what?"

"I've been using these databases longer than you have, Tom. I've got a pretty good idea where to hunt for certain types of files. Anyway, I took a look, and I found some interesting stuff—including the ship's passenger manifest." She reached out then and touched my cheek briefly. "I haven't looked at it, Tom. This is your business, not mine. I merely copied it over to a file and piped it over to the terminal in your quarters. It should be there now, if you want to look at it."

I stood motionless, stunned by what she'd said. Then, after a moment, I nodded again. "Thanks, Alex," I said. "I really appreciate this."

She held up her hand, cutting me off. "Hey," she said. "What are friends for?"

Sudden emotion churned up within me, and I felt my lips twitch into a smile that was half amusement and half pain. "Friends," I repeated, too softly for her to hear. She was right, though. We were that, and now that I had my future back, we had a chance of becoming more.

"Come on, friend," I said, and this time my smile held no pain at all. "Let's go see what you found."

Jamie was there when we came in. He took one look at my face and came up out of his bunk. "What's wrong, Tom?" he asked.

"Hey, buddy," I said, heading over to the terminal and motioning him to come with us. Alex was right behind me. "Come over here. I'd like you to see this."

"What is it?" he asked, but I didn't answer. He was coming over, and we'd all have the answer to that question soon enough.

My hands were shaking slightly as I sat down and pulled the keyboard closer to me. I wasn't sure what I would find when I accessed that file—and suddenly I wasn't so sure what I *wanted* to find.

"This is it," I said softly. Taking a deep breath, I reached out and hit the sequence of keys that would bring up the file.

Alex had been thorough in researching that ship. She'd learned that it had originally been christened *Passing Fancy*, but the name and serial numbers had all been removed at some point. Even without them, however, she had uncovered almost everything there was to know about it: where it had been built, who the captain was when they set off on that last fateful voyage, what kind of cargo was on board, even the date that they left. I glossed over all that, however. I wasn't interested in those kinds of details. Not yet, anyway. Not until I knew who had been on board.

The passenger list was at the very end of the file, and it was as complete as the rest. Each person's name was listed, along with their birth date, their previous address, their education and occupation, and more, all listed in dry, official report language. But it was all facts—no speculation on why any of them had joined this particular group, and no indication as to what had happened to them.

But we didn't need a report for that. We knew what had happened to them. It had been obvious from the moment that first pirate ship started its attack run.

There were two hundred forty-seven passengers on board that ship, but it didn't take me long to find what I was looking for. There, about three quarters of the way down the listing, was a family of three: George Chevalier, Amanda Wagner, and their son, Brian Chevalier, age fourteen at the time the ship departed their home world, Hopewell IV.

My hands froze, and then, almost as if they had a mind of their own, hit the keys that called up the file picture for the Chevalier family.

Behind me, Alex gave a little gasp, but she didn't say anything. At the same moment I felt Jamie's hand fall on my shoulder as he said, "My God, Tom! That's you!"

"I know," I said softly.

Emotions tore through me, a maelstrom of conflicting feelings—loss, joy, sadness, triumph, confusion, bitterness—all this and many more, less easily catalogued. I closed my eyes for a moment, letting myself drift on the storm of emotions.

"What is this, Tom?" Jamie asked. "Where did you get it?"

But I merely shook my head and stared at the picture on the screen. The man was tall, at least from what I could tell, with brown hair and soft brown eyes. The funny thing was that his picture, and the picture of the young me staring out from the screen, evoked no feelings within me. The two of them—my father and I—could have been total strangers for all that I recognized either of them. But the woman was a different story. She had auburn hair, and eyes of bright green, and when I looked into them I knew that I had known her. Sadness shot through me like a lightning bolt, sadness and loss and the sense that a part of me had suddenly been ripped away.

"Mother," I said, my fingers lightly brushing across the screen, as though I could reach through the glass and through the long, intervening years, to touch her one last time. But I couldn't, and after a moment I called up the records for fourteen-year-old Brian Chevalier.

I was a good student, I saw, a quiet kid with an avid interest in sports—something I had never been drawn to on Brighthome. One notation made me smile, if only briefly, however: on one aptitude test, I had written that I wanted to be a pilot someday. There was no mention of the Space Guard, but it pleased me to know that at least one of my original dreams had come true.

I knew what had happened, then, and again I felt myself overwhelmed by the surging tide of emotions. It was all so clear to me now. We had been aboard the *Passing Fancy*, bound for somewhere. Why we were on that ship was something I would never know. Perhaps my parents wanted to build a better life for me—or perhaps they were pursuing their own dreams, with no thought of the cost to their only child. My file said nothing about my friends, but I had to assume that I'd had some, and that leaving them was as hard for me as it would have been for any fourteen year old.

I wondered what they had thought—what I had thought—when the pirates started firing on their ship. The battle would have been quick, however. These were colonists, not warriors, and they would have been no match for the pirates.

I stopped myself from picturing what would have happened once the pirates boarded. I'd seen enough in the unrestricted files to have a good idea what kind of people these pirates were, and I didn't want to think about that happening to my father . . . or to my mother.

My own fate was a bit more curious, but again it was plain to see what had happened. I was too young for them to kill, but they couldn't just let me go—especially if they had used one or more of their stealth ships in the attack. They wouldn't have dared let me inform the Guard of their capabilities. So they did the only thing they could think of, and they probably thought they were doing me a favor: they brainwiped me, taking away all my conscious memories, leaving me with language and the ability to walk and with very little more. Then they put me in a survival pod and sent me on my way, to be discovered sometime later by a passing Guard ship.

Without my knowing it, my hands had formed themselves into fists. I was squeezing so tightly that I could feel my nails digging into my palms—not hard enough to draw blood, but hard enough that my fingers felt stiff as I forced them to relax.

Calling up the photo of my family once more, I felt the sting of unshed tears burning at my eyes.

"Tom," Jamie said. "What's going on? Who is Brian Chevalier?"

"No one," I said, and in that moment the surging tide of emotions crystallized within me into a single resolution, a decision so clear that I didn't have to even question it. "He's dead," I said.

Alex moved forward, then, coming up right behind me and resting her hand lightly on the back of my head.

She didn't say a word, but the comfort she offered with her touch meant a lot to me.

Jamie gripped my shoulder tightly. "But he's you," he said. "Brian Chevalier is you."

I shook my head. "Not any more," I said.

Slowly, I reached out and deleted the file that Alex had created for me.

"What are you doing?" Jamie cried as I hit the keys.

"Burying him," I said. At the last moment, however, I shunted the photo itself off to a separate file. I didn't need the records, not anymore, but someday I might want that picture. Someday I might be able to look at it again without crying.

"Tom," Jamie said, "I mean, Brian—"

I rose from my chair and spun to face him. Alex stepped back, giving me room.

"No," I said, cutting him off. "Whoever I was, whoever I might have been, my name is Tom, Tom Jenkins, and I'm a member of the Space Guard. That's all there is to it."

Jamie looked at me for a moment, his face solemn, and then he nodded.

Alex stood silently, her face awash with conflicting emotions. After a moment, though, she relaxed, and a slow smile slid across her features. Pulling herself erect, she gave me a salute and said, "Welcome home, Tom."

I smiled at her, and in that moment I knew, beyond any doubt, that I would wear down whatever reservations she had about the two of us. However long it took, I was determined that we would one day be much more than mere friends.

"Now come on," she said. "The captain said for you to report to the bridge when ready. He said to tell you this ship needs a pilot."

I was torn again. Part of me wanted to race to the bridge to resume my duties, but another part of me wanted to stay there, with Alex, to ask her about Ensign

Davies, to ask her about her feelings, to ask her about us. But that could wait, I realized. Thanks to the message she had brought from the review board, I had time once again, time to take things slowly, time to wait for her to come around.

I grinned again and returned her salute. "I'm ready now," I said. "Inform the captain that I'm on my way."

I turned away, secure in the knowledge that our future was safe once more. Whatever happened, whatever lay before us, we would meet it together, as a team, the way it should be.

Leaving my two best friends behind, I headed toward the bridge, and toward the future, to resume my duties once more.

Epilogue

Silently, it drifted through the blackness of space, no longer lifeless. Within its belly, ancient relays clicked over and banks of controls, dormant for eons, charged up and began functioning once more.

For millions of years, it had sent out a continuous signal, shining it on the underside of the fabric of space, where only The People could see it. This signal had been a beacon, summoning those who had needed help, and for the longest time it had gone unanswered.

Now it had been answered, but not by The People.

More circuits came alive, awakening even more banks of controls. Sensor analysis. Signal recording. Threat assessment. All this and more, things it had once known how to do but had almost forgotten in the long and silent years.

These were not The People, that it knew. Their ships were not ships of The People. Their weapons were not weapons of The People. And there was no signal from them, no answer to its call.

No, they were not The People, but they were not The Enemy, either. It could forget much through the long, dark passage of time, but it could never forget The People, and it could never forget The Enemy.

Most of all, though, it could never forget its mission.

The People were dead. It knew that, just as it knew that The Enemy was dead as well. Its first years of active service, like its last years of active service, had been on the fringes of the war, but it had followed the progress of the battles. The People had been slow to pick up their own weapons, slow to retaliate, slow to slip back into the ways of violence they had cast off long before; but once they did, once they put aside their hesitation and their inhibitions, they were formidable indeed.

By the close of the war, The Enemy had no planets left, just a few ships, manned and unmanned both, but The People were down to their last outpost.

The outpost did not survive. The Enemy threw everything they had at it, committed to taking The People down with them, and they succeeded. But not forever. For The People were dead, but The People would live again.

At least, that was the plan.

Its mission had been to rescue any of The People who were in need of help, to rescue them and to bring them back to the last remaining outpost in hopes of finding medical attention. But after the final confrontation its mission became its Purpose: to rescue The People as a whole, not just individually.

For The People still existed, inside their pocket universes, ready to emerge once more. For those who were injured, there would need to be medical facilities; for those who were dead, there would need to be a way to mine their genetic material so that The People would live once more.

To do that, however, it needed help. It needed a race that was neither The People nor The Enemy, with the technology to build what was needed. And now, for the first time in all the long and lonely years, it had found such a people. Their technology was still simple, lacking the tools to even open the pockets, much less help those inside, but they would learn. With its help, they would learn.

But first, it had to be sure of them. It could not afford a mistake. The People would have only one chance to live, a chance it did not dare to waste. It would watch, it would learn, and, when the time was right, it would act—or, better yet, it would allow this new people to act. But not until it was satisfied.

Shutting down its systems, it went dark and lifeless once more, drifting through the silence of space, waiting. . . .

DAVID WEBER

Honor Harrington (cont.):

Field of Dishonor

Honor goes home to Manticore—and fights for her life on a battlefield she never trained for, in a private war that offers just two choices: death—or a "victory" that can end only in dishonor and the loss of all she loves....

Other novels by DAVID WEBER:

Mutineers' Moon

"...a good story...reminds me of 1950s Heinlein..."
—*BMP Bulletin*

The Armageddon Inheritance

Sequel to *Mutineers' Moon*.

Path of the Fury

"Excellent...a thinking person's Terminator."
—*Kliatt*

Oath of Swords

An epic fantasy.

with STEVE WHITE:

Insurrection
Crusade

Novels set in the world of the Starfire ™ game system.

And don't miss Steve White's solo novels,
***The Disinherited** and **Legacy**!*

continued ☞

NEW FROM BAEN

IF YOU LIKE... YOU SHOULD TRY...

Norse Mythology... *The Mask of Loki* by
Roger Zelazny & Thomas T. Thomas

The Iron Thane by Jason Henderson

Sleipnir by Linda Evans

Puns... *Mall Purchase Night* by Rick Cook

The Case of the Toxic Spell Dump
by Harry Turtledove

Quests... *Pigs Don't Fly* and *The Unlikely Ones*
by Mary Brown

The Deed of Paksenarrion by Elizabeth Moon

Through the Ice by Piers Anthony & Robert Kornwise

Vampires... *Tomorrow Sucks*
by Greg Cox & T.K.F. Weisskopf